Pencilventure

Pencilventure:
The Ancient Forest Temple

R. J. F.

R. J. F.

Pencilventure: The Ancient Forest Temple
Player Sheet

Puzzle	Pencilventure: The Ancient Forest Temple Player Sheet	Your HP. /5 Enemy HP. /
Items Shrinking Pendant (a) Bow & Arrow (b) Sack of Food (c) Key (d) Key (e) Potion Potion Potion **Actions** Enter (1) Attack (2) Examine (3) Interact (4) Climb (5) **Combat** Attack Phase -Punch (Z) -Sword (Y) Defence Phase -Dodge (X) -Block (W) -Counter (V) Any Phase -Run (U)	Map	Notes

Adventurer Name: __________________________

Dear Player

Here is your handy-dandy Player Sheet (on your left). Now, even though you *could* write in the book, you really shouldn't. The pages of a tome are sacred and should be treated with the utmost respect … or something along those lines. As anyone who is used to gamebooks knows, the Player Sheet is printed here as a guide for you to copy onto another piece of paper. Please don't make a fool of yourself and write in the actual book. Have some decency.

Sincerely,

The Narrator

How to Play

Introduction

Hello and welcome to Pencilventure! If you are reading this, you are either super bored, really curious and have nothing better to do, or you've played gamebooks before and are reading this one entirely on purpose and completely unironically (I guess that's a possibility). Either way, I'll try to make it fun for you. "Who am I?" you ask? I'm the handy-dandy Narrator (obviously). "But, Narrator," I hear you saying, "what is this Pencilventure thing? Looks like some sort of game. Can I play? How do I play it? When will you give me answers?" Slow your roll (I don't get paid enough to hear you throw a tantrum).

Pencilventure is a pen(cil) and paper game that requires only four things to play: a pencil, an eraser, the Pencilventure Script (which is the thing you're reading), and the Pencilventure Player Sheet. I suppose if you have one of those fancy pencils with an eraser at the end, then you only really need three things. Lucky you! Oh, and it's imperative that you have a pencil, not a pen. You'll need to be able to rub things out.

Anyway, this is a game in which you must solve puzzles, navigate a labyrinth, and fight monsters in order to reach your goal. That's pretty much the gist of it, but let's go into more detail, shall we?

Playing the Game

You'll begin the game at the "Start" paragraph (the one immediately following the "How to Play" section). By reading that paragraph, you'll get a small description of where you are and what you're doing, then you'll be told to proceed to the "I" paragraph. This is how you will progress through the game, by reading the paragraph and moving on to one of many others (stick with me, it'll make more scenes soon). Let's look at an example paragraph.

I

Location: Room Sample. Sample Sample Sample why are you reading this? It's just a sample paragraph. Stop wasting time. Go to the next paragraph and continue learning how to play. Or don't, I don't own you, do what you want. You're not gonna read anything valuable here though. Not even if it's written in *italics* (II). It won't change a thing. Not even *this* (III) word will change anything. **Even though I'm in bold print now, it's still a waste of time reading this. Though I suppose there's no turning back now. So please, move on to the next paragraph.**

This is what a paragraph may look like in the game. The paragraphs will vary, but this should be good enough to give you an idea. So, starting at the top, we have the Paragraph Code (the bolded "I" at the top). All the paragraphs are marked with a unique code consisting of roman numerals, lower case letters, numbers, or a combination of the three. This is how the paragraphs are indentified and referenced. A paragraph may tell you to go to "IV" paragraph, or you may want to use an item, and to do so, you will need to go to "Vb" paragraph (more on that later). This system will help you navigate the paragraphs and know which paragraph you are supposed to read.

Next, Let's look at the parts of the paragraph written in **bold**. These parts are where important information is written. They can include your current location, which paragraph to read next, or inform you that you have obtained an item, among other things. Bolded text will often give you instructions on how to proceed so you don't scratch your head saying, "Wait, what am I supposed to do?"

The regular text in a paragraph is used to describe your surroundings and explain what is happening. Read it carefully, often clues to puzzle solutions are hidden in this text.

Lastly, the text written in *italics* with bracketed roman numerals next to them. These are things you can interact with. They could be doors, treasure chests, people, monsters, and so on. Using your Player Sheet, you can pair an Action or Item Code to the Interaction Code (the roman numerals next to the italicised word) in order to interact with that thing (more on this later).

Oh, almost forgot. Some paragraphs end with the words, "What do you do?". This indicates that it is time for you to pick an action to perform (more on this later).

All right, now you know the workings of a paragraph, let's look at progression using the Player Sheet.

Progressing Through the Game

Okay, let's talk about the Player Sheet and how to use it (you might want to be looking at your Player Sheet right now for context).

Puzzle Section

Right, starting from the top left we have the "Puzzle" section. This is used to write down your answers to any puzzles or riddles you may encounter. You don't have to write your answers down, this is just so you don't forget them in the time it takes for you to flip to the "Puzzle" section (not the one on the Player Sheet, a different one.

You'll figure it out soon) and check if your answer is correct.

Items Section

Below the last section is the "Items" section. This is a list of all the items in the game. When you start, you won't be able to use any of these items because you don't yet have them. You'll have to find them within the labyrinth. When you do find an item (signified in the bolded text of some paragraphs), draw a checkmark next to the corresponding item to signify that you have found it. Keys, potions, and the Sack of Food item are all perishable, meaning you can only use them once after having obtained them. (Perhaps put a little mark next to them on your Player Sheet to remind you of that.) If you use one of these items (e.g. a key), draw an X next to it to signify that you have used the item and cannot use it again.

To sum up, in some bolded texts you will be notified that you have obtained an item (let's say it's a key). When this happens, draw a checkmark next to the item you've obtained so you know that you've found the item. Perhaps you'll encounter a locked door that requires a key to open it. If you use the key you just obtained to unlock it, then you will have to draw an X next to the key so that you know you have already used the item and you cannot use it again.

Note that the Shrinking Pendant and Bow & Arrow items can be used as many times as you wish once you've obtained them.

Also, you may notice that there are two keys and three potions in the "Items" section. This is because there are more than one of these items in the game and it is possible to have more than one of them at a time.

Now you can keep track of all your items (you're welcome). "But wait," I hear you saying, "why do some of the items have letters next to them?" That's an excellent question. The letters (they look like this : "(a)", "(b)", etc.) indicate that the item can be used to interact with certain objects in the game. This is where the magic starts. Let's say you've found a key and you want to use it to open a locked door. How do you do that? Well, it's simple. The door is intractable (you can tell because it's written in italics), which means it has an Interaction Code (the roman numerals next to the word). Let's say the door's code is "IV". Now, you want to use your key to open it. The key has an Item Code (in this case "(d)"). So all you have to do is attach the key's code to the end of the door's code (i.e. IV + d = IVd). Now you have your completed code: "IVd". All you have to do now is find the paragraph with the code "IVd" (the Paragraph Code is the thing at the top of a paragraph, in case you forgot) (and don't worry, the paragraphs are in numerical order, so it shouldn't be hard to find). Once you've found the right paragraph, read it. It will tell you what happens by using the key to unlock the door. You can use this "code matching" method to use any item to interact with any object. Mix and match, see what happens, but remember, you can't do this with an item you don't already have; you must have found the item first.

Actions Section

All right, that's enough about Items, let's talk Actions (the section below Items). There are five actions (say 'em with me): Enter, Attack, Examine, Interact, and Climb. Most of these are self-explanatory but let's go through them anyway.

"Enter" lets you enter things like doors or anything really. You could enter a monster if you really wanted to, see what happens.

Next up is "Attack." This lets you attack whatever you want. Usually, using this will initiate the Combat Phase, but we'll get into that later.

"Examine" allows you examine any particular thing more closely. You might want to do this when you need more information about something you've stumbled upon (it's a good way to get hints).

"Interact" often does the same thing as "Examine," but, depending on what you're interacting with, the "Interact" option could allow you to talk to another character, or push a button, or something like that.

Lastly, there's the "Climb" action. You use this to climb things (maybe that's obvious).

Now, you've probably noticed that the Actions have numbers next to them. If you're really smart, then you've already figured out what they do, but we'll go over it anyway (not all of you are ahead of the class. I've got to look out for the dumb ones too). Like the "Items" before, the "Actions" have their own codes too, which you add to the end of the Interaction Code of an object in order to perform an action on said object. For example, if you wanted to enter a door, you would take the door's code ("VI"), then add the code for "Enter" ("1") and get "VI1". You would then find the "VI1" paragraph and that would tell you what happens by your entering the door. You can attach any Action Code to any Interaction Code, so try them out and see what happens.

Combat Section

Next we have Combat (below Actions). We'll talk more about this later, but essentially these are the actions you'll use to defend yourself in a fight.

Map Section

The big section in the middle is the Map section. This is where you'll draw your map. It is a labyrinth after all, so having a good map is the key to not getting lost. You can draw your map however you like, but remember to mark down the locations of objects inside rooms, so you know where they are. To make things easier, assume that you are always facing North (you can even write an "N" at the top of the map). So if a paragraph tells you that there is a door in front of you, it is to the North. If there is a door on your left, it is to the west. Got it? (For those of you thinking it would be easier to use compass directions rather than left, right, in front, and behind, I did try bringing that up to *her*, but she wouldn't have it. She doesn't like her rules being bent and she pays the bills so I didn't argue the point.)

Paragraphs that tell you your location will help you know what room you are in, and in turn, that will help you name the rooms you'll draw in your map. Here are some map-drawing tips: the labyrinth is big, so start the map at the bottom centre and leave space between rooms; if an object is written with italics, you should probably draw it into the map so you don't forget it's there; don't forget to draw all the doors in their proper locations (remember: you're always facing north); and also, don't forget to make a distinction between locked doors and unlocked doors; a good way to make a comprehensive map is to make it simple. Just make every room a circle and connect them together with lines. And don't forget to write down the names of the rooms, that's important.

HP Section

Next is the HP section (top right). HP is your health. You start with a total of five HP, but if you drop to zero, you'll lose and have to start the game over (or at a checkpoint, more on that later).

You can go ahead and write a five in the empty space next to "Your HP." This marks how much HP you have. If you lose HP, you'll have to subtract it from this number and then write in the new number. So if you have five HP and you take one damage, then you'll rub out the five and replace it with a four. If you hit zero, that's game over.

Are you wondering what can make you lose HP? Well, if you get hit by an enemy attack, that'll definitely put a hurt on you. But you can also lose HP for giving incorrect answers to puzzles, so be careful. It's not all doom and gloom though. You see those potions in the "Items" section? Those are hidden somewhere within the labyrinth. If you find one, you can use it at any time to regain one HP (remember when you use one to draw an X next to it to mark it as used. It's one use only).

Even though you can regain HP with potions, you can never have more than five HP (Why? Because *she* said it was really hard to get this game balanced and she won't have you messing it up. And I like my job, so I didn't argue). Also, I know I said you can use potions anytime, but that's not entirely true. The only time you can't use a potion is during a battle, because you'll be too busy fighting to down a potion (or the real reason, it would break the balance of the game).

Oh yeah, almost forgot, below "Your HP" is "Enemy HP." When you are fighting an enemy, you can keep track of their HP here, in the same way you keep track of your own. An enemy's HP can vary though, so you'll have to write in both numbers this time. We'll talk more about enemies and fighting later on. We've got one thing left.

Notes Section

The "Notes" section. This is where you take notes of everything important that happens. The game will tell you when and on what to take notes. This could range from noting that you've found an item, to noting that you've defeated an enemy.

Even though you'll be told what to note, you're not limited to this. If you think something's important, note it, so you can remember it. You never know when things will come in handy.

Oh, and the "Adventurer Name" section is where your name goes (if that wasn't obvious).

Checkpoints

Checkpoints are points in the game from which you can restart if you run out of HP. When you find a checkpoint, you will be informed of this through bolded text in a paragraph. In this text, you will be asked to draw a horizontal line after all your notes in the "Notes" section of the Player Sheet. This acts as a save point; everything before the line is saved and will remain if your HP hits zero, but everything you may add after the line will be lost if you hit zero. For example, let's say you find a potion and a checkpoint. You would then draw a horizontal line after all your notes (including the one stating that you've found a potion). Now after this, you unlock a door and fight an enemy, but you lose the fight, and your HP drops to zero. You will be able to start again from the room in which you found the checkpoint, and everything before the line you drew (i.e. the potion you found) is safe and remains unchanged (even if you used the potion after finding the checkpoint, you'll get it back and be able to use it again, so long as the note of your using it was written after the horizontal line, or in other words, after you found the checkpoint). However, everything noted after the line (i.e. the door you unlocked) will need to be erased as it is now lost and you'll have to do it over again. Also, when you return to a checkpoint after hitting zero HP, your HP will be fully replenished to five. And lastly, checkpoints will last forever. You can lose multiple times, but you'll always be able to return to the last checkpoint. (That being said, you can only get each individual checkpoint once. You can't just go back to the same room over and over to infinitely save your progress. That's cheating. I know you were thinking about it.)

(Also, friendly tip, note down the paragraph you got the checkpoint in, so you remember where to return to if you die. You're welcome.)

Combat

All right, so how exactly does Combat work? When a battle with an enemy begins (sometimes this is automatic and sometimes you initiate it by matching your Attack Code ("3") to an enemy's Interaction Code (e.g. "VII"), you will be told through bolded text to go to the "Enemy Combat" section corresponding to the monster you are fighting. Once there, you'll be told what you're fighting and how much HP it has (at this time, you would write the enemy's HP in the "Enemy HP" section of the Player Sheet). You will also be reminded how combat works so you can effectively fight the enemy.

Now, battles are split up into rounds, which are split into two phases: Attack Phase and Defence Phase. During the Attack Phase, you'll be presented with three paragraphs (don't read them yet). These paragraphs will be marked as Z, Y, and U. You may notice that Z, Y, and U also appear on your Player Sheet in the "Combat" section. That is because these are your options for fighting the enemy. Basically, you decide what you want to do ("Punch", "Sword", or "Run") then read the corresponding paragraph to see what happens.

These paragraphs are a little different from others as the important parts are in the regular text, not the bolded text (although, for all paragraphs it's important to read everything). Within the regular text, you'll find how much damage you've dealt or taken. You will use this information to calculate how much remaining HP both you and your enemy have (using the HP sections on the Player Sheet to help keep track). For example, perhaps you strike with your sword and deal two damage, you will then subtract two from the enemy's HP and write the remainder in the "Enemy HP" section. The bolded parts of these paragraphs will tell you which paragraph to read in order to continue the battle. You'll continue like this until either you or the enemy hits zero HP. If you hit zero first, then you lose and will have to start the whole game over (or from a checkpoint if you've found one). If the enemy is the first to hit zero, then you've successfully defeated it and you will be asked to write this in the "Notes" section of the Player Sheet (and if you both hit zero at the same time, you lose). When the battle concludes, you can return to the rest of the game by going to the paragraph that you were told to go to at the beginning of the battle if you were to win.

The Defence Phase works the same as the Attack Phase, except you'll be using the Defence Phase options instead of the Attack Phase options. You'll alternate between the two phases during battle; the Attack Phase being focused more on dealing damage, and the Defence Phase being more focused on trying not to take damage. Let's take a closer look at all your options.

The "Punch" option is a weak attack, but it comes with a chance of stunning an enemy. Why would you want to do that? Well, some enemy can go into what's called Swift Mode. When this happens, the enemy will be stronger, more agile, and generally harder to defeat. However, if you can land a punch before this happens, you can prevent the enemy from entering Swift Mode.

The "Sword" option lets you attack with your sword (yes, you have a sword. Don't let it go to your head). It's great for dealing a good amount of damage, but some monsters have a resistance to it.

The "Dodge" option allows you to avoid an enemy's attack. It doesn't work very well on fast enemies though.

The "Block" option allows you to block an incoming attack, but this won't work well on strong enemies.

The "Counter" option lets you block an attack and strike back as well, but be careful, this doesn't work well on all enemies, you may find yourself on the receiving end of their own counter.

Lastly, the "Run" option allows you to run from a battle without having defeated the enemy and return to the paragraph indicated by the bolded text in the "U" paragraph (in case you don't think you're hero enough to survive the fight). Sometimes, running can be a good thing (live to fight another day, right?), but some enemies are really good at trapping an opponent, and if you try to run from them, you'll be unsuccessful and take damage.

Now, let's say you're fighting an enemy. You damage it a little and then you decide to run. If you return to this fight again, it will start over from the beginning and the enemy will again have full HP (that's just how the cookie crumbles). You, on the other hand, will have no such luxury. Your HP will never replenish automatically. You'll have to replenish it with potions (but remember, you can't use a potion during a battle, only before or after the battle).

So as a recap, you use the Attack Phase options during the Attack Phase, the Defence Phase options during the Defence Phase, and you can use the "Run" option at any time (but remember, don't read any of the paragraphs that don't correspond to the option you choose during the battle … that would be cheating).

"But, hang on," you may be wondering, "how can I tell what works best against which enemies? How do I know if an enemy is fast or strong? How can I know when an enemy is about to enter Swift Mode?" Well, in-between each round, there'll be a short paragraph detailing my thoughts on the battle so far and (if you're lucky) some words of encouragement. In those paragraphs, you may find hints to help you determine how best to fight your enemy … if you're looking for them. Here's an example of what the "Enemy Combat" section looks like:

Round 1: Attack

Okay, this thing looks big, you might want to hit it with something strong. What do you do?

Z

Ouch, is your hand okay? Maybe punching it wasn't such a good idea. You deal zero damage. **Apply any changes to HP and move on to "Round 1: Defence."**

Y

Good hit! Definitely have to clean that sword later though. You deal one damage. **Apply any changes to HP and move on to "Round 1: Defence."**

U

You try to run, but the enemy blocks your path and swipes at you. You take one damage. **Apply any changes to HP and move on to "Round 1: Defence."**

One more thing, fighting takes a lot of energy, and if you're tired, you won't do as well. With this in mind, it's best to defeat an enemy in the earlier rounds rather than the later rounds. As you grow more tired, your attacks will grow weaker, but monsters can fight a lot longer than you can. Just be careful, okay?

Conversations

Throughout your adventure you may stumble upon some other characters (what, you thought you were alone?). By using the "Interact" option on your Player Sheet (with the same code matching method used for everything else), you can start a conversation with any character you meet. When you do this, you will be told through bolded text to go to the "Conversations" section corresponding to the character you're talking to.

Conversations are easy. All you have to do is read what the character says (aka the "Start" paragraph [in the "Conversations" section, not the one at the beginning of the game]), and then read over your possible responses (listed alphabetically). Once you've decided which response you're going to use (e.g. Response A), read the character's "A" response. From there, you'll have a new set of responses from which to choose (e.g. A1, A2, A3). Pick one and read the corresponding response. Continue this process until the conversation is done. Here's an example of what a conversation might look like:

Start

"Oh no," the woman says. "I seem to have misplaced it."

Your Responses

A

Say, "What did you lose?"

B

Say, "Do you need help with something?"

C

Say, "Good luck finding whatever you're missing."

Woman's "A" response

"I seem to have lost my hat." She looks at you. "I wonder if you would help me find it?"

Woman's "B" response

"Why yes, I do … if you're offering.

Woman's "C" response

The woman sighs, "It would have been nice of you to help me, but I suppose nice people died out a long time ago."

You may be wondering what the point of conversations is; what do you get out of it? Well, aside from companionship, you can get information, or even items, but it all depends on what you say. Don't expect to just pick any response and arrive at the same conclusion, you'll have to choose your words wisely.

Puzzles

The "Puzzles" section is pretty straight forward. While playing the game you will encounter many puzzles that will require solutions. All you have to do is come up with the solution (write it down in the "Puzzle" section on the Player Sheet if you think you'll forget it) and check the corresponding puzzle in the "Puzzles" section (this one's in the book you're holding, not the Player Sheet one [confusing, right?]). There, you will find the correct answer and a paragraph telling you what to do. The rest will be explained when you get there.

Conclusion

All right, I think that's everything. Confused yet? Don't worry about it, it'll click when you're playing (plus the bolded text in the paragraphs are basically free reminders of the rules). There's a couple things you want to keep in mind though: don't neglect your map, a good map is the difference between being lost and knowing exactly where you are; also don't forget to write notes, if it seems important, then you should probably note it; don't forget to draw a checkmark or X when you obtain or use items respectively; remember, you can use a potion you've found at anytime to regain one HP except during a battle (don't break the game, *she's* worked hard to make it balanced, and I need this job).

And that's that! You're all set. When you're ready to get going, begin at the "Start" paragraph following this section. Oh, and, just so you know, given the nature of this game, you can decide to do some pretty odd things like climb a door or enter a key. Just know that if you choose one of these stupid options, I'll have to narrate it regardless. You may not think so, but I do have a life. I have a wife and two kids, and I really don't want to be here forever telling you for the millionth time that you can't enter a key. And if you're thinking that you're gonna do that now just to spite me, well … just remember who your friends are, 'cause you won't find many here.

P.S.

Are you thinking, "Man, I wish this game had a cool theme song I could listen to while I'm playing."? Well, it's your lucky day because there is a Pencilventure theme song. To hear it, go to YouTube and search for Pencilventure. It's the one titled "Pencilventure" with the book's cover image as the thumbnail (yes, I was paid extra to say that. I have a family to provide for).

Pencilventure: The Ancient Forest Temple

Start

You arrive at an old, weathered temple. There are cracks in its stony walls, and from those cracks, there are plants prospering in the soft sunlight and breaking through the leafy shield of the tall trees in the forest. In the past, this Ancient Forest Temple may have been a grand example of breathtaking architecture. But the truth lies in its title; the temple is ancient. Had you not heard about this place from some of the folk back in town, you might have walked past it thinking it was just a rocky cliff (it's that weathered). But here is the real question: why are you here? Well, those same townsfolk told you about an ancient treasure inside this ancient temple. They agreed to pay quite the sum of money if you could retrieve it for them. As an adventurer who loves money, you dashed straight for the temple, and now, here you are. Let's get started! **Continue to "I" paragraph.**

I

Location: Entrance. You are in a large, open area full of exotic plants. Straight ahead there is a *door* (II). Next to the door, there is a *stone tablet* (III) with writing etched into it. To your right, there are *vines* (IV) growing up a tree. A glimmer of light sparkles from the top of this tree. What do you do?

II1

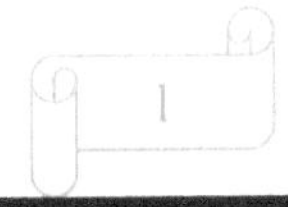

The door is locked. You'll need a key to open it. **If you have already unlocked this door, go to "V" paragraph. Otherwise, return to "I" paragraph.**

II2

Why would you attack a door? What did it do to you? **Return to "I" paragraph.**

II3

The door is locked. You'll need a key to open it. **If you have already unlocked this door, then it is unlocked. Return to "I" paragraph.**

II4

The door is locked. You'll need a key to open it. **If you have already unlocked the door, then it is unlocked. Return to "I" paragraph.**

II5

You want to climb a door? How? **Return to "I" paragraph.**

IIa

No effect. **Return to "I" paragraph.**

IIb

No effect. **Return to "I" paragraph.**

IIc

No effect. **Return to "I" paragraph.**

IId

You unlocked the door. **Mark this in "Notes" and draw an X next to the used item. If you have already unlocked the door, then this item has no effect. Return to "I" paragraph.**

IIe

You unlocked the door. **Mark this in "Notes" and draw an X next to the used item. If you have already unlocked the door, then this item has no effect. Return to "I" paragraph.**

III1

Enter … a stone tablet? You're joking, right? **Return to "I" paragraph.**

III2

It's not wise to attack random things. **Return to "I" paragraph.**

III3

You examine the stone tablet. It reads: "An elf's favourite colour is red." What do you suppose that means? **Return to "I" paragraph.**

III4

You examine the stone tablet. It reads: "An elf's favourite colour is red." What do you suppose that means? **Return to "I" paragraph.**

III5

You want to climb the stone tablet? Why, so you can be taller? Be serious. **Return to "I" paragraph.**

IIIa

No effect. **Return** to "I" paragraph.

IIIb

No effect. **Return** to "I" paragraph.

IIIc

No effect. **Return** to "I" paragraph.

IIId

No effect. **Return** to "I" paragraph.

IIIe

No effect. **Return** to "I" paragraph.

IV1

Don't be silly, you can't enter vines. **Return to "I" paragraph.**

IV2

You want to attack the vines? After they've committed the oh-so-terrible act of doing nothing? Do you know what a tree hugger is? Maybe you should look into it. **Return to "I" paragraph.**

IV3

These vines look pretty strong. They could probably hold your weight. **Return to "I" paragraph.**

IV4

These vines look pretty strong. They could probably hold your weight. **Return to "I" paragraph.**

IV5

You climb the vines to the top of the tree. Wow, there's a key up here, result! You take the key and climb back down the vines. **You obtained a key! Mark this in "Notes" and draw a checkmark next to the item. If you have already obtained this key, then you get nothing and you climb down disappointed. Return to "I" paragraph.**

IVa

No effect. **Return to "I" paragraph.**

IVb

No effect. **Return to "I" paragraph.**

IVc

No effect. **Return to "I" paragraph.**

IVd

No effect. **Return to "I" paragraph.**

IVe

No effect. **Return to "I" paragraph.**

V

A bat attacks you. I guess it's time to fight. **Continue to "Enemy Combat: "Bat" (page 70). If you have already defeated the bat, continue to "VI" paragraph.**

VI

Location: Room A. You walk into a circular room. You can see hints of stone or concrete scattered about, but most of it is engulfed in moss. To your left, there is a *door* (VII). Straight ahead, there is another *door* (VIII). Behind you there is yet another *door* (IX). What do you do? **You have reached the "Room A Checkpoint." Mark this in "Notes." Draw a horizontal line at the end of your notes. Everything written before this line has been saved, so if you are defeated, you can try again from this point with your HP fully restored to five (HP is only restored if you are defeated and return to a checkpoint; it is not restored now). Anything that happens after obtaining this checkpoint will be lost if you are defeated, and you will have to do those parts over again.**

VII1

It's open. You proceed to the next room. **Continue to "X" paragraph.**

VII2

Violence is never the answer … at least, not now. **Return to "VI" paragraph.**

VII3

The door is open. **Return to "VI" paragraph.**

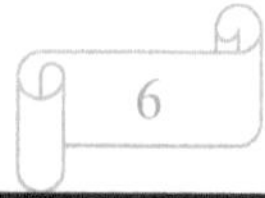

VII4

The door is open. **Return to "VI" paragraph.**

VII5

Climb a door? When you figure out how that works, come tell me. **Return to "VI" paragraph.**

VIIa

No effect. **Return to "VI" paragraph.**

VIIb

No effect. **Return to "VI" paragraph.**

VIIc

No effect. **Return to "VI" paragraph.**

VIId

No effect. **Return to "VI" paragraph.**

VIIe

No effect. **Return to "VI" paragraph.**

VIII1

It's open. You proceed to the next room. **Continue to "XIII" paragraph.**

VIII2

I don't think that's such a good idea, do you? **Return to "VI" paragraph.**

VIII3

The door is open. **Return to "VI" paragraph.**

VIII4

The door is open. **Return to "VI" paragraph.**

VIII5

Good for you, you can climb. If you want to show off, join a climbing club. **Return to "VI" paragraph.**

VIIIa

No effect. **Return to "VI" paragraph.**

VIIIb

No effect. **Return to "VI" paragraph.**

VIIIc

No effect. **Return to "VI" paragraph.**

VIIId

No effect. **Return to "VI" paragraph.**

VIIIe

No effect. **Return to "VI" paragraph.**

IX1

It's open. You walk through to the next room. **Continue to "I" paragraph.**

IX2

Do you think the options through before you select one? **Return to "VI" paragraph.**

IX3

The door is open. **Return to "VI" paragraph.**

IX4

The door is open. **Return to "VI" paragraph.**

IX5

And you'll gain what from doing this? **Return to "VI" paragraph.**

IXa

No effect. **Return to "VI" paragraph.**

IXb

No effect. **Return to "VI" paragraph.**

IXc

No effect. **Return to "VI" paragraph.**

IXd

No effect. **Return** to "VI" paragraph.

IXe

No effect. **Return** to "VI" paragraph.

X

Location: Room B. You are in a secluded area with glistening light shining from above. In front of you stands a large, purple *ostrich* (XI). It seems to be in distress. To your right there is a *door* (XII). What do you do?

XI1

I don't even want to know where you plan to enter an ostrich from. Just … no, you're not allowed. **Return to "X" paragraph.**

XI2

Whoa, whoa, whoa! You want to attack this poor, defenceless, ostrich. How cruel! Make it a rule to only attack scary, creepy, or ugly creatures, such as spiders or giant lizards. You're kind of racist that way, but, such is life. **Return to "X" paragraph.**

XI3

The ostrich has its head down. It seems to be in some sort of pain. Maybe if you interact with it, you could help it out … or not. Your choice. **Return to "X" paragraph.**

XI4

You approach the ostrich. **Go to "Conversations: Ostrich" (page 101).**

XI5

You attempt to climb atop the ostrich, but it gives you a piercing grimace that reaches into your soul, plucking away at it ever so slowly. You think that maybe this isn't such a good idea, as you desperately try not to pee your pants. **Return to "X" paragraph.**

XIa

No effect. **Return to "X" paragraph.**

XIb

You would shoot a defenceless ostrich with an arrow? Do you need a timeout? Save your exterminate-with-extreme-prejudice tendencies for the real enemies … like bats. You know what I'm talking about. **Return to "X" paragraph.**

XIc

You give the ostrich your sack of food. It gulps it down with just one bite and unleashes a loud, smelly belch. "Thank you," it says. "My stomach doesn't hurt anymore. I shall always remember this kindness. Do you think … this makes us friends?" The ostrich sports a gratuitous smile. **You and the ostrich have become friends. Mark this in "Notes." Draw an X next to the "Sack of Food" item. Return to "X" paragraph.**

XId

No effect. **Return to "X" paragraph.**

XIe

No effect. **Return to "X" paragraph.**

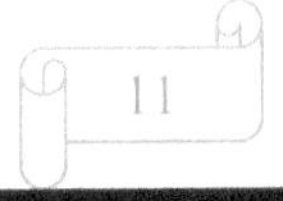

XII1

It's open. You walk through to the next room. **Go to "VI" paragraph.**

XII2

Don't waste your time attacking doors, it's embarrassing. Think of the children. What do you mean "What children?" Don't question me. Do you even know who I am? … Exactly, didn't think so. No, I am not The Narrator, although, that is my job (and how I introduced myself to you). Just … stop questioning me and play the game. Oh, great, you made me break the fourth wall. **Return to "X" paragraph.**

XII3

The door is open. **Return to "X" paragraph.**

XII4

The door is open. **Return to "X" paragraph.**

XII5

Ha, ha, ha, ha, ha, ha … wait, you're serious? No, you can't climb the door. **Return to "X" paragraph.**

XIIa

No effect. **Return to "X" paragraph.**

XIIb

No effect. **Return to "X" paragraph.**

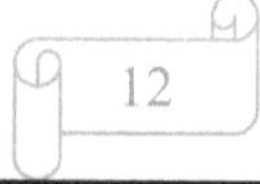

XIIc

No effect. **Return to "X" paragraph.**

XIId

No effect. **Return to "X" paragraph.**

XIIe

No effect. **Return to "X" paragraph.**

XIII

Location: Room C. You are in a large, foggy room, which, frankly, kind of smells. At your feet, there are numbers etched into the stone floor. "2, 4, 3, 1," that is what they say. I wonder what that's all about. To your left, there is a *door* (XIV). Straight ahead, there is a *door* (XV). To your right, there is a small *hole* (XVI) with rats scurrying in and out of it. Behind you, there is a *door* (XVII). What do you do?

XIV1

The door is open. You walk through to the next room. **Go to "XXI" paragraph.**

XIV2

I've heard that attacking doors is illegal in some places. You wouldn't be the hero if you broke the law, now, would you? **Return to "XIII" paragraph.**

XIV3

The door is open. **Return to "XIII" paragraph.**

XIV4

The door is open. **Return to "XIII" paragraph.**

XIV5

You climbed the door and found a mysterious rock … not. I don't know if you've realised, but, it's a door. How are you supposed to climb it? **Return to "XIII" paragraph.**

XIVa

No effect. **Return to "XIII" paragraph.**

XIVb

No effect. **Return to "XIII" paragraph.**

XIVc

No effect. **Return to "XIII" paragraph.**

XIVd

No effect. **Return to "XIII" paragraph.**

XIVe

No effect. **Return to "XIII" paragraph.**

XV1

The door is locked. You'll need a key to open it. **If you have already unlocked this door, go to "XLV" paragraph. If not, return to "XIII" paragraph.**

XV2

If you need something to test your sweet moves on, might I suggest an actual enemy and not a boring old door. Just a thought. **Return to "XIII" paragraph.**

XV3

The door is locked. You'll need a key to open it. **Return to "XIII" paragraph.**

XV4

The door is locked. You'll need a key to open it. **Return to "XIII" paragraph.**

XV5

If you're thinking that because the door is locked you'll be able to climb it … you're wrong. **Return to "XIII" paragraph.**

XVa

No effect. **Return to "XIII" paragraph.**

XVb

No effect. **Return to "XIII" paragraph.**

XVc

No effect. **Return to "XIII" paragraph.**

XVd

You unlocked the door. **Mark this in "Notes." Draw an X next to this item. If you have already unlocked this door, then this item has no effect, and you needn't draw an X next to the item. Return to "XIII" paragraph.**

XVe

You unlocked the door. **Mark this in "Notes." Draw an X next to this item. If you have already unlocked this door, then this item has no effect, and you needn't draw an X next to the item. Return to "XIII" paragraph.**

XVI1

The hole is too small to enter, you won't fit. **Return to "XIII" paragraph.**

XVI2

You'll never find this treasure if you swing your sword at everything you see. Time is precious, you know. **Return to "XIII" paragraph.**

XVI3

It's a small hole with rats scurrying in and out of it. You'll never fit through it, but the rats don't seem to have a problem. If only you were the size of a rat. **Return to "XIII" paragraph.**

XVI4

It's a small hole with rats scurrying in and out of it. You'll never fit through it, but the rats don't seem to have a problem. If only you were the size of a rat. **Return to "XIII" paragraph.**

XVI5

Have you ever tried to climb a small hole? Put this game down, go try it, and then come back and tell me how it went. Sigh, there goes the fourth wall. **Return to "XIII" paragraph.**

XVIa

You hold out the Shrinking Pendant, and slowly, the world around you begins to grow … no, it's you who are shrinking! These rats are much more menacing now. They're the size of bears … although, their horrendous case of overbite makes it a bit hard to take them seriously. Luckily for you, the rats are friendly. They stand on their hind legs and point to the hole. You walk in. Why not, right? **Go to "XVIII" paragraph.**

XVIb

No effect. **Return to "XIII" paragraph.**

XVIc

No effect. **Return to "XIII" paragraph.**

XVId

No effect. **Return to "XIII" paragraph.**

XVIe

No effect. **Return to "XIII" paragraph.**

XVII1

It's open. You walk through to the next room. **Go to "VI" paragraph.**

XVII2

What if you stupidly attacked the door and then your sword broke in two. Wouldn't that be embarrassing? Good thing I'm here to stop you from doing that sort of thing, right? **Return to "XIII" paragraph.**

XVII3

The door is open. **Return to "XIII" paragraph.**

XVII4

The door is open. **Return to "XIII" paragraph.**

XVII5

You know, I'm not paid by the hour to narrate this, so please don't waste my time. **Return to "XIII" paragraph.**

XVIIa

No effect. **Return to "XIII" paragraph.**

XVIIb

No effect. **Return to "XIII" paragraph.**

XVIIc

No effect. **Return to "XIII" paragraph.**

XVIId

No effect. **Return to "XIII" paragraph.**

XVIIe

No effect. **Return to "XIII" paragraph.**

XVIII

Location: Room D. You return to regular size. A small room surrounds you. The room is bright and inviting, however, there is a skeleton on the ground. That's not creepy at all … yeah, right. To your left, there is a small *hole* (XIX). To your right, there is a shiny, golden basin filled with a *blue liquid* (XX). What do you do?

XIX1

The hole is too small for you to enter. If only you were the size of a rat. **Return to "XVIII" paragraph.**

XIX2

Did you know that swords can get blunt? They don't stay sharp forever, but they'll remain sharp for longer so long as you don't waste their integrity on something dumb, like a small hole. **Return to "XVIII" paragraph.**

XIX3

The hole has rats scurrying in and out of it, but you're too large to get through. If only you were the size of a rat. **Return to "XVIII" paragraph.**

XIX4

The hole has rats scurrying in and out of it, but you're too large to get through. If only you were the size of a rat. **Return to "XVIII" paragraph.**

XIX5

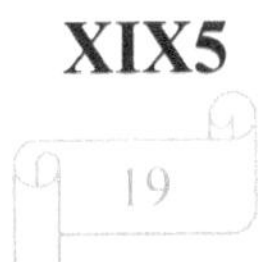

You're going to climb a hole? … Okay, quick question, how? I'll give you some time to think … you good now? Good. Now let's leave the stupidity behind and keep trucking along. **Return to "XVIII" paragraph.**

XIXa

You hold out the Shrinking Pendent, and slowly, you shrink … obviously. And then, off you go, through the … rat-hole. Why do I want to say rabbit-hole? Weird. **Go to "XIII" paragraph.**

XIXb

No effect. **Return to "XVIII" paragraph.**

XIXc

No effect. **Return to "XVIII" paragraph.**

XIXd

No effect. **Return to "XVIII" paragraph.**

XIXe

No effect. **Return to "XVIII" paragraph.**

XX1

Well, I don't know. It's a basin of blue liquid, you don't know what it is. Maybe you could enter it and end up in some fantastical world, but I'll just save you the time and use my other-worldly powers to tell you that the only thing you'll get from entering the basin is wet. **Return to "XVIII" paragraph.**

XX2

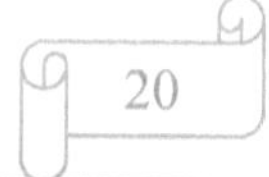

You know, a long time ago—well before you were born—humans used to attack everything that they did not understand. Long story short, they all died. Maybe following in their footsteps isn't the best idea. Unless you see a monster, in which case, stab your sword right through its heart and watch the blood drip from its corps. Mwahaha! … Er, forget I said that. **Return to "XVIII" paragraph.**

XX3

You peer into the basin and see the glistening, blue liquid housed within. This may be your eyes deceiving you, but you think you can see some sort of writing within the water. It says: "Pool of Healing. One sip, and your troubles shall wash away." **Return to "XVIII" paragraph.**

XX4

You cup your hand in the liquid, bring it to your mouth, and drink. It tastes … bitter. It's kind of slimy too … gross! **If this is your first time drinking this liquid, mark this in "Notes" and go to "XXf" paragraph. If you have drunk this liquid before, go to "XXg" paragraph.**

XX5

No, no, don't do that. The basin's probably slippery. What if you fall and break your back? Then you won't find the treasure, and—more importantly—you won't get paid. Foresight, it's a good skill to have. What would you do without me? Stop complaining, I'm not oppressing you, I'm saving you. **Return to "XVIII" paragraph.**

XXa

No effect. **Return to "XVIII" paragraph.**

XXb

No effect. **Return to "XVIII" paragraph.**

XXc

No effect. **Return to "XVIII" paragraph.**

XXd

No effect. **Return to "XVIII" paragraph.**

XXe

No effect. **Return to "XVIII" paragraph.**

XXf

You start to feel a tingling sensation, otherwise known as "feelin' the healin'." You feel pretty good now. But then you hear a shrill voice in your head. "Who said you could drink from my basin? You greedy little human. How dare you? Never come back here, do you hear me? No matter how badly you need the healing properties of my liquid, never, ever, return." **You regain 2 HP from the liquid. Mark that you have drunk from the pool in "Notes." Return to "XVIII" paragraph.**

XXg

You wait patiently for your healing to begin, but it doesn't. Instead, you feel a little sick. A shrill voice appears in your head. "I told you not to come back here, you greedy human. Now you get what you and all your kind deserves." The voice disappears with a menacingly shrill laugh. **You lose 2 HP from the effects of the liquid. Return to "XVIII" paragraph.**

XXI

Location: Room E. You are in a small room with a bit more stone in it than greenery. Blood stains the floor and walls. Straight ahead, there is a *door* (XXII), but it is blocked by a *giant lizard* (XXIII) about twice your size. To your right, there is a *door* (XXIV). What do you do? **If you have already defeated the giant lizard, then it is no longer here.**

XXII1

The door is block by the giant lizard. You cannot enter. **If you have already defeated the giant lizard, the door is no longer blocked, and you enter it. Proceed to "XXV" paragraph. If you have not yet defeated the giant lizard, return to "XXI" paragraph.**

XXII2

You want to attack the door? Okay, let me just ask the door if that's okay … the door said "no." Guess you're out of luck. **Return to "XXI" paragraph.**

XXII3

The door is open. **Return to "XXI" paragraph.**

XXII4

The door is open. **Return to "XXI" paragraph.**

XXII5

You seriously want to climb a door? Okay, that's it, I'm done. You hear me? I quit. Find someone else to narrate this rubbish! …

Um … they offered to up my pay, so I'm back. But please don't say anything stupid again. **Return to "XXI" paragraph.**

XXIIa

No effect. **Return to "XXI" paragraph.**

XXIIb

No effect. **Return to "XXI" paragraph.**

XXIIc

No effect. **Return to "XXI" paragraph.**

XXIId

No effect. **Return to "XXI" paragraph.**

XXIIe

No effect. **Return to "XXI" paragraph.**

XXIII1

I don't know where or how you plan to enter a giant lizard, but if you do, you will die. Trust me. There will be a funeral—which I will not attend—and there will be a tombstone that will read: "here lies Stupid, the one who tried to enter a giant lizard, and paid the ultimate price." **Return to "XXI" paragraph.**

XXIII2

You lock eyes with the giant lizard. No words are exchanged—not because lizards can't talk, but because at this moment, the only language you speak is battle (and maybe a little bit because lizards can't talk). Do me a favour and don't die. I'll be out of a job if you do! **Continue to "Enemy Combat: Giant Lizard" (page 79).**

XXIII3

It's a giant lizard—maybe a gecko. It's about twice your size, though it remains on all fours. There is blood dripping from its mouth. It doesn't seem that you'll be able to get past it without a fight. **Return to "XXI" paragraph.**

XXIII4

It's a giant lizard—maybe a gecko. It's about twice your size, though it remains on all fours. There is blood dripping from its mouth. It doesn't seem that you'll be able to get past it without a fight. **Return to "XXI" paragraph.**

XXIII5

You can try, but I'm not going to pick up your pieces when you're done. **Return to "XXI" paragraph.**

XXIIIa

No effect. **Return to "XXI" paragraph.**

XXIIIb

No effect. **Return to "XXI" paragraph.**

XXIIIc

No effect. **Return to "XXI" paragraph.**

XXIIId

No effect. **Return to "XXI" paragraph.**

XXIIIe

No effect. **Return to "XXI" paragraph.**

XXIV1

It's open. You walk through to the next room. **Go to "XIII" paragraph.**

XXIV2

Do people attack doors where you're from? No? Then why would you think it's a good idea to do that here? Do you feel the shame? Good. Let's move on. **Return to "XXI" paragraph.**

XXIV3

The door is open. **Return to "XXI" paragraph.**

XXIV4

The door is open. **Return to "XXI" paragraph.**

XXIV5

As much as we'd like to, sometimes you just can't do whatever a spider can. **Return to "XXI" paragraph.**

XXIVa

No effect. **Return to "XXI" paragraph.**

XXIVb

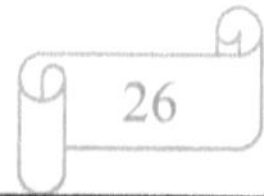

No effect. **Return to "XXI" paragraph.**

XXIVc

No effect. **Return to "XXI" paragraph.**

XXIVd

No effect. **Return to "XXI" paragraph.**

XXIVe

No effect. **Return to "XXI" paragraph.**

XXV

Location: Room F. You are in a room of untamed greenery; it almost looks like outside. To your left, there is a *door* (XXVI). Straight ahead, there is a *door* (XXVII) with four *buttons* (XXVIII) on it. The buttons are numbered from one to four. Behind you, there is a *door* (XXIX). What do you do?

XXVI1

The door is open. You walk through to the next room. **Go to "XXX" paragraph.**

XXVI2

You move to attack the door, but it roars at you ferociously and you back away … just kidding. Wouldn't that be funny, though? **Return to "XXV" paragraph.**

XXVI3

The door is open. **Return to "XXV" paragraph.**

XXVI4

The door is open. **Return to "XXV" paragraph.**

XXVI5

Don't say stupid things like that, or else I'll call in a bunch of monsters and end this game early. I have a life you know. Even though I'm just The Narrator, that doesn't mean I don't have a say in what goes down. I happen to be *her* quaternary best friend (if you know what I mean). **Return to "XXV" paragraph.**

XXVIa

No effect. **Return to "XXV" paragraph.**

XXVIb

No effect. **Return to "XXV" paragraph.**

XXVIc

No effect. **Return to "XXV" paragraph.**

XXVId

No effect. **Return to "XXV" paragraph.**

XXVIe

No effect. **Return to "XXV" paragraph.**

XXVII1

The door seems to be locked; it won't budge. **If you have already completed the button puzzle, go through to the next room, "XXXIII" paragraph. If not, return to "XXV" paragraph.**

XXVII2

Whoa, what are you doing? Put your sword away and repeat after me, "Doors are friends, not targets." **Return to "XXV" paragraph.**

XXVII3

The door appears to be locked, yet there is no keyhole. What could unlock the door if not a key? There are four numbered buttons on the door. Maybe the right combination will open it. But what could the combination be? **Return to "XXV" paragraph.**

XXVII4

The door appears to be locked, yet there is no keyhole. What could unlock the door if not a key? There are four numbered buttons on the door. Maybe the right combination will open it. But what could the combination be? **Return to "XXV" paragraph.**

XXVII5

If you like climbing so much, then why not go rock climbing in real life, rather than trying to climb a door in a game? **Return to "XXV" paragraph.**

XXVIIa

No effect. **Return to "XXV" paragraph.**

XXVIIb

No effect. **Return to "XXV" paragraph.**

XXVIIc

No effect. **Return to "XXV" paragraph.**

XXVIId

No effect. **Return to "XXV" paragraph.**

XXVIIe

No effect. **Return to "XXV" paragraph.**

XXVIII1

I know this is just a game to you, and you want to pick stupid options just to see what I'll say, but please, have mercy. I have to stay here until you either die or find the treasure, and you really don't want me rooting for the wrong side ... I have influence. **Return to "XXV" paragraph.**

XXVIII2

You can't attack buttons. Why? Because no one scripted that option. It's stupid. **Return to "XXV" paragraph.**

XXVIII3

There are four numbered buttons. There might be some sort of code you need to punch in to open the door. **Return to "XXV" paragraph.**

XXVIII4

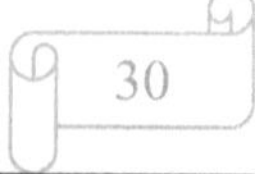

You push the buttons and enter a code. **Write your four-digit code in the "Puzzle" section of your Player Sheet. The buttons are numbered 1, 2, 3, and 4, and you may only push each button once. Once you have come up with a code to try, check your answer in the "Puzzles: Button Puzzle" section (page 109).**

XXVIII5

If you can figure out how to climb buttons, then maybe you should be narrating and I should be playing. **Return to "XXV" paragraph.**

XXVIIIa

No effect. **Return to "XXV" paragraph.**

XXVIIIb

No effect. **Return to "XXV" paragraph.**

XXVIIIc

No effect. **Return to "XXV" paragraph.**

XXVIIId

No effect. **Return to "XXV" paragraph.**

XXVIIIe

No effect. **Return to "XXV" paragraph.**

XXIX1

The door is open. You walk through to the next room. **Go to "XXI" paragraph.**

XXIX2

Don't be paranoid. You haven't even opened the door yet and you're already trying to kill it. Control yourself. **Return to "XXV" paragraph.**

XXIX3

The door is open. **Return to "XXV" paragraph.**

XXIX4

The door is open. **Return to "XXV" paragraph.**

XXIX5

Does someone need a psychiatric evaluation? **Return to "XXV" paragraph.**

XXIXa

No effect. **Return to "XXV" paragraph.**

XXIXb

No effect. **Return to "XXV" paragraph.**

XXIXc

No effect. **Return to "XXV" paragraph.**

XXIXd

No effect. **Return to "XXV" paragraph.**

XXIXe

No effect. **Return to "XXV" paragraph.**

XXX

Location: Room G. You walk into a small room. It's quite spacious, complete with some torches, a table and chair, and various other household items. In the centre of the room stands an *old man* (XXXI). To your right, there is a *door* (XXXII). What do you do?

XXXI1

No, no, I'm not letting you do that. I'm not even going to say it. Why? Because it's gross! Think about it … Talk about an accidental euphemism. This is not that sort of game. **Return to "XXX" paragraph.**

XXXI2

Attacking the elderly in against the law … Yes, it is! Don't argue with me. **Return to "XXX" paragraph.**

XXXI3

It's an old, wrinkly man. He seems to be quite happy though. He's giving you a strange look, like he wants to speak to you. But you would have to start the conversation of course. Not everyone is as socially inclined as are you. **Return to "XXX" paragraph.**

XXXI4

You strike up a conversation with the old man, using your sweet conversational skills. **Go to "Conversations: Old Man" (page 106).**

XXXI5

He's too old and frail to be able to carry you so there's not much to gain from, uh, climbing him. Maybe we should just forget you said that. Deal? **Return to "XXX" paragraph.**

XXXIa

No effect. **Return to "XXX" paragraph.**

XXXIb

That's rude! **Return to "XXX" paragraph.**

XXXIc

He's not hungry. No, I didn't ask him. Yes, I'm sure he's not hungry. I used my mind-reading powers, okay? Stop asking me questions; I'm just The Narrator. **Return to "XXX" paragraph.**

XXXId

No effect. **Return to "XXX" paragraph.**

XXXIe

No effect. **Return to "XXX" paragraph.**

XXXII1

The door is open. **Go to "XXV" paragraph.**

XXXII2

If you're looking for an epic battle, find a monster to slay, not a door. **Return to "XXX" paragraph**

XXXII3

The door is open. **Return to "XXX" paragraph.**

XXXII4

The door is open. **Return to "XXX" paragraph.**

XXXII5

Hey, are you a climber or an adventurer? You can't be both. Yes, I realise you technically are both, but your primary goal is adventuring … because I said so. Don't fight me on this. **Return to "XXX" paragraph.**

XXXIIa

No effect. **Return to "XXX" paragraph.**

XXXIIb

No effect. **Return to "XXX" paragraph.**

XXXIIc

No effect. **Return to "XXX" paragraph.**

XXXIId

No effect. **Return to "XXX" paragraph.**

XXXIIe

No effect. **Return to "XXX" paragraph.**

XXXIII

Location: Room H. You are in a room filled with enormous spider webs. To your left, there is a *door* (XXXIV). Straight ahead, there is a *door* (XXXV), but it is blocked by a huge *spider* (XXXVI). Behind you, there is a *door* (XXXVII) What do you do?

XXXIV1

You walk through the door and proceed to the next room. **Go to "XXXVIII" paragraph.**

XXXIV2

Really? Do you really think that's a good idea? **Return to "XXXIII" paragraph.**

XXXIV3

The door is open. **Return to "XXXIII" paragraph.**

XXXIV4

The door is open. **Return to "XXXIII" paragraph.**

XXXIV5

Why do you say such silly things? **Return to "XXXIII" paragraph.**

XXXIVa

No effect. **Return to "XXXIII" paragraph.**

XXXIVb

No effect. **Return to "XXXIII" paragraph.**

XXXIVc

No effect. **Return to "XXXIII" paragraph.**

XXXIVd

No effect. **Return to "XXXIII" paragraph.**

XXXIVe

No effect. **Return to "XXXIII" paragraph.**

XXXV1

The door is blocked by a giant spider. It won't let you pass. **If you have already defeated the spider, then you enter to the next room. Go to "XLI" paragraph. Otherwise, return to "XXXIII" paragraph.**

XXXV2

Don't you think there's a better use of your time. **Return to "XXXIII" paragraph.**

XXXV3

The door is open, but it is blocked by a giant spider. **Return to "XXXIII" paragraph.**

XXXV4

The door is open, but it is blocked by a giant spider. **Return to "XXXIII" paragraph.**

XXXV5

Yeah, I don't think so. **Return to "XXXIII" paragraph.**

XXXVa

No effect. **Return to "XXXIII" paragraph.**

XXXVb

No effect. **Return to "XXXIII" paragraph.**

XXXVc

No effect. **Return to "XXXIII" paragraph.**

XXXVd

No effect. **Return to "XXXIII" paragraph.**

XXXVe

No effect. **Return to "XXXIII" paragraph.**

XXXVI1

Enter … a spider? Ha ha ha ha ha! **Return to "XXXIII" paragraph.**

XXXVI2

You whip out your blade and yell, "Have at thee!" … Weirdo. **Go to "Enemy Combat: Spider" (page 87). If you have already** defeated the spider, then it is no longer here, **and, since there's nothing to attack, return to "XXXIII" paragraph.**

XXXVI3

Whoa, that is a big, hairy, ugly spider. Why is it winking at you? Or maybe it can't blink all its eyes at once. Gross! **Return to "XXXIII" paragraph.**

XXXVI4

Whoa, that is a big, hairy, ugly spider. Why is it winking at you? Or maybe it can't blink all its eyes at once. Gross! **Return to "XXXIII" paragraph.**

XXXVI5

Well, I guess you *could* ride the giant spider and trample everything in your path, but it's far more likely that the spider will just eat you, so … **Return to "XXXIII" paragraph.**

XXXVIa

No effect. **Return to "XXXIII" paragraph.**

XXXVIb

You ready your bow and fire. Wow, I … I think it's dead. Well, that was quick. **You've defeated the spider. Mark this in your "Notes." Return to "XXXIII" paragraph.**

XXXVIc

No effect. **Return to "XXXIII" paragraph.**

XXXVId

No effect. **Return** to "XXXIII" paragraph.

XXXVIe

No effect. **Return** to "XXXIII" paragraph.

XXXVII1

You walk through the door and proceed to the next room. **Go to "XXV" paragraph.**

XXXVII2

Are you okay? You know a door won't hurt you, right? This isn't like that one temple in which some doors are wobbly and will fall on top of you … What? You've never played that game before? **Return to "XXXIII" paragraph.**

XXXVII3

The door is open. **Return to "XXXIII" paragraph.**

XXXVII4

The door is open. **Return to "XXXIII" paragraph.**

XXXVII5

In order to climb, you kind of need something to hold on to. I just don't think you'll find that kind of help from a door. **Return to "XXXIII" paragraph.**

XXXVIIa

No effect. **Return** to "XXXIII" paragraph.

XXXVIIb

No effect. **Return to "XXXIII" paragraph.**

XXXVIIc

No effect. **Return to "XXXIII" paragraph.**

XXXVIId

No effect. **Return to "XXXIII" paragraph.**

XXXVIIe

No effect. **Return to "XXXIII" paragraph.**

XXXVIII

Location: Room I. You are in a small room. It's sort of cold … in a ghostly way. On the walls there is some sort of *mysterious writing* (XXXIX). To your right, there is a *door* (XL). What do you do?

XXXIX1

Typically, writing is not on the list of things one can enter. I'd love to make an exception, but I don't what to. **Return to "XXXVIII" paragraph.**

XXXIX2

You know, words are considered a nonviolent way to get one's point across. Perhaps you should give that a go some time. **Return to "XXXIII" paragraph.**

XXXIX3

You examine the writing. It says, "What is an elf's favourite colour?" **Come up with your answer now and write it in the "Puzzle" section of the Player Sheet. Then, go to "Puzzles: Mysterious Writing" (page 111) to check your answer.**

XXXIX4

You examine the writing. It says, "What is an elf's favourite colour?" **Come up with your answer now and write it in the "Puzzle" section of the Player Sheet. Then, go to "Puzzles: Mysterious Writing" (page 111) to check your answer.**

XXXIX5

You can't do that. Why not? Don't ask me, ask whoever invented physics. **Return to "XXXIII" paragraph.**

XXXIXa

No effect. **Return to "XXXIII" paragraph.**

XXXIXb

No effect. **Return to "XXXIII" paragraph.**

XXXIXc

No effect. **Return to "XXXIII" paragraph.**

XXXIXd

No effect. **Return to "XXXIII" paragraph.**

XXXIXe

No effect. **Return to "XXXIII" paragraph.**

XL1

You walk through to the next room. **Go to "XXXIII" paragraph.**

XL2

I could come up with something clever to say here, but I'm just going to let you figure out for yourself why you can't do that. **Return to "XXXIII" paragraph.**

XL3

The door is open. **Return to "XXXIII" paragraph.**

XL4

The door is open. **Return to "XXXIII" paragraph.**

XL5

Were you a gecko in a past life? You certainly have that same affinity for climbing. Sorry to break it to you, but human hands don't really work that way. **Return to "XXXIII" paragraph.**

XLa

No effect. **Return to "XXXIII" paragraph.**

XLb

No effect. **Return to "XXXIII" paragraph.**

XLc

No effect. **Return to "XXXIII" paragraph.**

XLd

No effect. **Return to "XXXIII" paragraph.**

XLe

No effect. **Return to "XXXIII" paragraph.**

XLI

Location: Room J. You are in quite a rugged and rocky room. It's a little hard to walk around due to the tough terrain, but you'll survive. Strangely, in midair floats a stony *gargoyle head* (XLII). In the centre of the room, there is a *treasure chest* (XLIII). Behind you, there is a *door* (XLIV). What do you do?

XLII1

It's not a portal to another world, it's a gargoyle head. How are you going to enter it? **Return to "XLI" paragraph.**

XLII2

It's floating too high for you to reach with your sword. Hmm … **Return to "XLI" paragraph.**

XLII3

It's a floating gargoyle head. Not moving, just floating. It has its mouth open. Maybe something will happen if you put something in it (get your mind out of the gutter). Although, there's no way you'll reach it with your sword (I said out of the gutter). Hmm, I wonder what you should do. **Return to "XLI" paragraph.**

XLII4

It's a floating gargoyle head. Not moving, just floating. It has its mouth open. Maybe something will happen if you put something in it (get your mind out of the gutter). Although, there's no way you'll reach it with your sword (I said out of the gutter). Hmm, I wonder what you should do. **Return to "XLI" paragraph.**

XLII5

It's too high up for you to even attempt to climb it—and for the record, you can't climb the wall to get to the gargoyle head. I hate to lay out restrictions, but if I don't, this game will be more broken than the fourth day. What? You don't know that reference? Well, aren't you lucky the moon doesn't have a face? **Return to "XLI" paragraph.**

XLIIa

No effect. **Return to "XLI" paragraph.**

XLIIb

You ready your bow and fire at the gargoyle head. Upon being struck dead in the mouth, the head disappears, and something falls from the sky into your hands. It's a pendant of some kind. It looks to be made entirely out of gold. It has a blue centre that almost seems more liquid than solid, but not so much that it could be poured out onto the floor; it's more like jelly. When you wrap the pendant around your neck, you hear a strange voice: "You are now in possession of the Shrinking Pendant. Use it wisely." **You have obtained the Shrinking Pendant. Mark this in "Notes" and draw a checkmark next to the item. If you have already obtained the Shrinking Pendant, then you may not obtain a second one. Return to "XLI" paragraph.**

XLIIc

No effect. **Return** to "XLI" paragraph.

XLIId

No effect. **Return** to "XLI" paragraph.

XLIIe

No effect. **Return** to "XLI" paragraph.

XLIII1

In this world, we don't enter treasure chests. **Return to "XLI" paragraph.**

XLIII2

I can't let you do that. What if there's a wicked security system? I mean, there probably isn't, but … just don't attack it, okay? **Return to "XLI"** paragraph.

XLIII3

It's a treasure chest, and it seems to be unlocked. I wonder if there's something inside. **Return to "XLI" paragraph.**

XLIII4

You open the treasure chest and find a key! **You obtained a key. Mark this in "Notes" and draw a checkmark next to the item. If you have already obtained this key, then you can't have another one. Return to "XLI" paragraph.**

XLIII5

You could do that, but … why? **Return to "XLI" paragraph.**

XLIIIa

No effect. **Return to "XLI" paragraph.**

XLIIIb

No effect. **Return to "XLI" paragraph.**

XLIIIc

No effect. **Return to "XLI" paragraph.**

XLIIId

No effect. **Return to "XLI" paragraph.**

XLIIIe

No effect. **Return to "XLI" paragraph.**

XLIV1

You enter the door and go through to the next room. **Go to "XXXIII" paragraph.**

XLIV2

This is no time for jokes, you have a treasure to find. **Return to "XLI" paragraph.**

XLIV3

The door is open. **Return to "XLI" paragraph.**

XLIV4

The door is open. **Return to "XLI" paragraph.**

XLIV5

Wasn't there a movie where the first guy to die in the squad was the climbing guy? Best to not follow his example. **Return to "XLI" paragraph.**

XLIVa

No effect. **Return to "XLI" paragraph.**

XLIVb

No effect. **Return to "XLI" paragraph.**

XLIVc

No effect. **Return to "XLI" paragraph.**

XLIVd

No effect. **Return to "XLI" paragraph.**

XLIVe

No effect. **Return to "XLI" paragraph.**

XLV

Location: Room K. This room is small and foggy. You don't know why, but something in your gut tells you that you are getting close to the treasure. Call it "adventurer's instinct;" after all, this is what you do for a living. Straight ahead, there is a *door* (XLVI). On that door, is a set of two *buttons* (XLVII). To your right, there is a *door* (XLVIII). Behind you, there is a *door* (XLIX). What do you do?

XLVI1

The door won't budge. How did I know it wasn't going to be that easy? **If you have already unlocked this door, go to "LIV" paragraph, otherwise, return to "XLV" paragraph.**

XLVI2

I'm just going to ignore you, because I know that you know that attacking a door is utter nonsense. **Return to "XLV" paragraph.**

XLVI3

The door appears to be locked. There's no keyhole either. Hmm … then, how do we open it? **Return to "XLV" paragraph.**

XLVI4

The door appears to be locked. There's no keyhole either. Hmm … then, how do we open it? **Return to "XLV" paragraph.**

XLVI5

You know how in some games you can climb almost any surface? (Unless it's raining). This is not one of those games. **Return to "XLV" paragraph.**

XLVIa

No effect. **Return to "XLV" paragraph.**

XLVIb

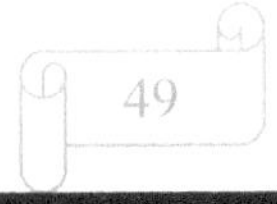

No effect. **Return to "XLV" paragraph.**

XLVIc

No effect. **Return to "XLV" paragraph.**

XLVId

No effect. **Return to "XLV" paragraph.**

XLVIe

No effect. **Return to "XLV" paragraph.**

XLVII1

Dude, they're buttons, you can't enter them. **Return to "XLV" paragraph.**

XLVII2

No, wait! Think about this. What if the buttons are … booby trapped? Although, there doesn't seem to be any other way to open the door, so you'll have to see what the buttons do. Still, be gentle. Not everything has to meet the edge of your sword. **Return to "XLV" paragraph.**

XLVII3

There are two buttons on the door: 1 and 2. Maybe one of them opens the door, but which one? **Return to "XLV" paragraph.**

XLVII4

You walk up to the buttons and ponder the coming decision. Which one should you press? **Decide which button you are**

going to press (1 or 2), then check your answer by going to "Puzzles: Switch Puzzle" (page 113).

XLVII5

When we're done here, would you like to be a monkey? They can climb whatever they want. Wouldn't you like that? Well, you've got to find this treasure as a human first, then we can talk about species transition. **Return to "XLV" paragraph.**

XLVIIa

No effect. **Return to "XLV" paragraph.**

XLVIIb

No effect. **Return to "XLV" paragraph.**

XLVIIc

No effect. **Return to "XLV" paragraph.**

XLVIId

No effect. **Return to "XLV" paragraph.**

XLVIIe

No effect. **Return to "XLV" paragraph.**

XLVIII1

The door is open, and you go through to the next room. **Go to "L" paragraph.**

XLVIII2

That doesn't sound very productive. **Return to "XLV" paragraph.**

XLVIII3

The door is open. **Return to "XLV" paragraph.**

XLVIII4

The door is open. **Return to "XLV" paragraph.**

XLVIII5

What do you know, you climbed the door … somehow. I'm messing with you, let's just keep moving. **Return to "XLV" paragraph.**

XLVIIIa

No effect. **Return to "XLV" paragraph.**

XLVIIIb

No effect. **Return to "XLV" paragraph.**

XLVIIIc

No effect. **Return to "XLV" paragraph.**

XLVIIId

No effect. **Return to "XLV" paragraph.**

XLVIIIe

No effect. **Return to "XLV" paragraph.**

XLIX1

The door is open. You proceed to the next room. **Go to "XIII" paragraph.**

XLIX2

Think of all the famous adventurers you know. Do any of them attack harmless doors? Yeah, I didn't think so. **Return to "XLV" paragraph.**

XLIX3

The door is open. **Return to "XLV" paragraph.**

XLIX4

The door is open. **Return to "XLV" paragraph.**

XLIX5

Are you really trying to climb a door? Stop that, before someone sees. You're being an idiot. **Return to "XLV" paragraph.**

XLIXa

No effect. **Return to "XLV" paragraph.**

XLIXb

No effect. **Return to "XLV" paragraph.**

XLIXc

No effect. **Return to "XLV" paragraph.**

XLIXd

No effect. **Return to "XLV" paragraph.**

XLIXe

No effect. **Return to "XLV" paragraph.**

L

Location: Room L. You are in a small, almost secretive room. You feel a little cold, but you'll survive. Don't be a wimp. In the middle of the room, there is a *brown sack* (LI) with something inside. To your left, there is a *door* (LII). To your right, there is a strange *gargoyle statue* (LIII) with its mouth open. It sort of looks … hungry? Strange. What do you do?

LI1

Let's not be silly now. **Return to "L" paragraph.**

LI2

It's a brown sack. It's not attacking you, so why would you attack it? **Return to "L" paragraph.**

LI3

It's a brown sack. There seems to be something inside. Hmm, I wonder what. **Return to "L" paragraph.**

LI4

You pick up the sack and look inside. It seems to be full of breadcrumbs. I doubt a sack of breadcrumbs will fill you, but maybe you can use it for something else. **You obtained the Sack**

of Food. Mark this in "Notes" and draw a checkmark next to the item. If you have already obtained this item, you cannot obtain another one. Return to "L" paragraph.

LI5

I can't even imagine how that would be remotely possible. Did I forget to mention that the sack is small? **Return to "L" paragraph.**

LIa

No effect. **Return to "L" paragraph.**

LIb

No effect. **Return to "L" paragraph.**

LIc

No effect. **Return to "L" paragraph.**

LId

No effect. **Return to "L" paragraph.**

LIe

No effect. **Return to "L" paragraph.**

LII1

The door is open. You proceed to the next room. **Go to "XLV" paragraph.**

LII2

Are you doing this because you think it's funny? I do have a life, you know. It's not my fault I'm only qualified to guide idiots, uh … I mean adventurers through this game. Give me a break. **Return to "L" paragraph.**

LII3

The door is open. **Return to "L" paragraph.**

LII4

The door is open. **Return to "L" paragraph.**

LII5

If you want to climb, then climb. When you're done, we can get back to the game. **Return to "L" paragraph.**

LIIa

No effect. **Return to "L" paragraph.**

LIIb

No effect. **Return to "L" paragraph.**

LIIc

No effect. **Return to "L" paragraph.**

LIId

No effect. **Return to "L" paragraph.**

LIIe

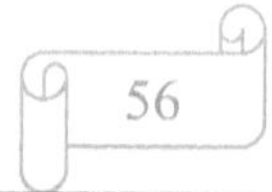

No effect. **Return to "L" paragraph.**

LIII1

Where do you plan on entering from? Its mouth may be open, but it's too small for you to fit. Besides, do you honestly think you'll gain anything from doing that? **Return to "L" paragraph.**

LIII2

You swing your sword and strike the statue, but nothing happens. You should really be more careful. It's not uncommon for inanimate objects to come to life when attacked. I know you think that I'm here to guide you and that I won't put you in harm's way—that is my job, after all—however, I never said I was any good at my job. Makes you think twice, doesn't it? **Return to "L" paragraph.**

LIII3

It's a gargoyle statue with its mouth open. It kind of looks … hungry? Maybe you could try feeding it. You never know what could happen. Although, why would you feed a statue? There's probably a better use of your time and resources. **Return to "L" paragraph.**

LIII4

It's a gargoyle statue with its mouth open. It kind of looks … hungry? Maybe you could try feeding it. You never know what could happen. Although, why would you feed a statue? There's probably a better use of your time and resources. **Return to "L" paragraph.**

LIII5

The statue is quite angular, it will be hard to climb it. But, perhaps more importantly, why would you climb it? **Return to "L" paragraph.**

LIIIa

No effect. **Return to "L" paragraph.**

LIIIb

Jeez, you're lucky it's just a statue, that would've really hurt. Don't be so mean. **Return to "L" paragraph.**

LIIIc

You place the Sack of Food in the statue's mouth. The mouth slowly closes, and then slowly opens, but now, there is something new inside. The Sack of Food is gone, but it has been replaced with a potion. **You obtained a potion. Mark this in your "Notes" and draw a checkmark next to the item. You have also lost the Sack of Food. Mark this in your "Notes" and draw an X next to the item. Return to "L" paragraph.**

LIIId

No effect. **Return to "L" paragraph.**

LIIIe

No effect. **Return to "L" paragraph.**

LIV

Location: Room M. You are in a cold room. The floor is laced with a purple fog. How mysterious. Wait, what's that? You hear a voice in your head. It says: "Dear adventurer, soon, you will be faced with some challenging riddles. Though I cannot answer them for you, I can tell you this: riddles are to be taken literally." Huh, what do you suppose that means? Oh well, let's continue. To your left, there are some *vines* (LV). Straight ahead, there is a *door* (LVI) from which the purple fog seems to be coming. Behind you, there is a *door* (LVII). What do you do? **You have reached a checkpoint. Mark this in "Notes." Draw a horizontal line at the end of your notes. Everything written before this line has been saved, so if you are defeated, you can try again from this point with your HP fully restored to five (HP is only restored if you are defeated and return to the checkpoint; it is not restored now). Anything that happens after obtaining this checkpoint will be lost if you are defeated, and you will have to do those parts again.**

LV1

Vines are not among the many things you may enter in the game. **Return to "LIV" paragraph.**

LV2

Are the vines hurting you? No. So why, pray tell, would you even consider hurting them? **Return to "LIV" paragraph.**

LV3

It seems the vines lead to somewhere, but you can't see where from where you stand. **Return to "LIV" paragraph.**

LV4

It seems the vines lead to somewhere, but you can't see where from where you stand. **Return to "LIV" paragraph.**

LV5

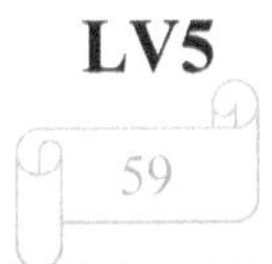

You climb up the vines. **Go to "LVIII" paragraph.**

LVa

No effect. **Return to "LIV" paragraph.**

LVb

No effect. **Return to "LIV" paragraph.**

LVc

No effect. **Return to "LIV" paragraph.**

LVd

No effect. **Return to "LIV" paragraph.**

LVe

No effect. **Return to "LIV" paragraph.**

LVI1

The door is open. You proceed to the next room. **Go to "LXIV" paragraph.**

LVI2

Oh, you say such funny things. **Return to "LIV" paragraph.**

LVI3

The door is open. **Return to "LIV" paragraph.**

LVI4

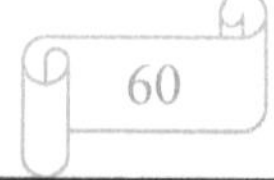

The door is open. **Return to "LIV" paragraph.**

LVI5

Wait, I sense something. I sense … that there may be something else nearby that may satisfy your climbing needs. Maybe you should climb whatever that is and not the door. **Return to "LIV" paragraph.**

LVIa

No effect. **Return to "LIV" paragraph.**

LVIb

No effect. **Return to "LIV" paragraph.**

LVIc

No effect. **Return to "LIV" paragraph.**

LVId

No effect. **Return to "LIV" paragraph.**

LVIe

No effect. **Return to "LIV" paragraph.**

LVII1

The door is open. You proceed to the next room. **Go to "XLV" paragraph.**

LVII2

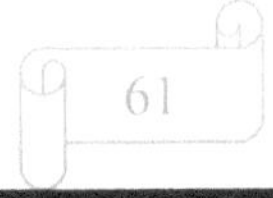

You cannot do that, please understand. **Return to "LIV" paragraph.**

LVII3

The door is open. **Return to "LIV" paragraph.**

LVII4

The door is open. **Return to "LIV" paragraph.**

LVII5

I don't think I'm comfortable with you doing that. **Return to "LIV" paragraph.**

LVIIa

No effect. **Return to "LIV" paragraph.**

LVIIb

No effect. **Return to "LIV" paragraph.**

LVIIc

No effect. **Return to "LIV" paragraph.**

LVIId

No effect. **Return to "LIV" paragraph.**

LVIIe

No effect. **Return to "LIV" paragraph.**

LVIII

Location: Atop the vines. You are on a small, rocky ledge. There doesn't seem to be much going on up here; what a shame. However, there is a very small *hole* (LIX) near your feet. It's way too small for you to crawl through though. I suppose there's nothing left to do but climb back down the *vines* (LX).

LIX1

The hole is much too small for you to enter. **Return to "LVIII" paragraph.**

LIX2

Well, you could try, but I'm telling you now, it won't do anything. **Return to "LVIII" paragraph.**

LIX3

The hole is quite small. If you could only shrink down to a smaller size, maybe then you could get through. **Return to "LVIII" paragraph.**

LIX4

The hole is quite small. If you could only shrink down to a smaller size, maybe then you could get through. **Return to "LVIII" paragraph.**

LIX5

You can barely fit your hand through the hole, how do you expect to climb it? **Return to "LVIII" paragraph.**

LIXa

You shrink down to the size of a rat (any smaller and I'll get a copyright claim), and then, you walk through the hole. **Go to "LXI" paragraph.**

LIXb

No effect. **Return to "LVIII" paragraph.**

LIXc

No effect. **Return to "LVIII" paragraph.**

LIXd

No effect. **Return to "LVIII" paragraph.**

LIXe

No effect. **Return to "LVIII" paragraph.**

LX1

Now, you know … that I know … that you know … that I know … that you know you can't do that. **Return to "LVIII" paragraph.**

LX2

I feel like you already know what I'm going to say. **Return to "LVIII" paragraph.**

LX3

They're vines; nothing special about them. **Return to "LVIII" paragraph.**

LX4

They're vines; nothing special about them. **Return to "LVIII" paragraph.**

LX5

You climb down the vines. **Go to "LIV" paragraph.**

LXa

No effect. **Return to "LVIII" paragraph.**

LXb

No effect. **Return to "LVIII" paragraph.**

LXc

No effect. **Return to "LVIII" paragraph.**

LXd

No effect. **Return to "LVIII" paragraph.**

LXe

No effect. **Return to "LVIII" paragraph.**

LXI

Location: Room N. You are in a very small room. As you return to regular size, the smallness grows much more apparent. But hey, you still fit … result! In the centre of the room, there is a *potion* (LXII). To the right, there is a small *hole* (LXIII). What do you do?

LXII1

You understand that potions are contained in small bottles, right? And even if you were small enough to somehow enter the bottle, you would drown in the liquid. Just forget it. **Return to "LXI" paragraph.**

LXII2

When we're done here, you should have that paranoia issue of yours checked out. **Return to "LXI" paragraph.**

LXII3

It's a potion. They're good to have around as they can heal your wounds, but remember, you can't use them in battle. Why? Because you're battling, there's no time to drink potions, duh! **Return to "LXI" paragraph.**

LXII4

You take the potion. **You have obtained a potion. Mark this in your "Notes" and draw a checkmark next to the item. If you have already obtained this potion, then you may not have another one. Return to "LXI" paragraph.**

LXII5

Climb a potion? Now does that make sense to you? Let's be reasonable. **Return to "LXI" paragraph.**

LXIIa

No effect. **Return to "LXI" paragraph.**

LXIIb

No effect. **Return to "LXI" paragraph.**

LXIIc

No effect. **Return to "LXI" paragraph.**

LXIId

No effect. **Return to "LXI" paragraph.**

LXIIe

No effect. **Return to "LXI" paragraph.**

LXIII1

I don't even think you could get your foot in there, let alone your whole body. **Return to "LXI" paragraph.**

LXIII2

You don't attack the hole, the hole attacks you … make of that what you will. **Return to "LXI" paragraph.**

LXIII3

Is this not the same hole you came in from? Do you really need to examine it again? Ugh, fine. It's a small hole. You probably won't be able to fit in it. If only you were smaller. I'd better be getting paid overtime for this. **Return to "LXI" paragraph.**

LXIII4

Is this not the same hole you came in from? Do you really need to examine it again? Ugh, fine. It's a small hole. You probably won't

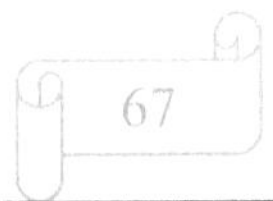

be able to fit in it. If only you were smaller. I'd better be getting paid overtime for this. **Return to "LXI" paragraph.**

LXIII5

Look, I know some games promote creativity and out-of-the-box thinking—and to an extent, this is one of those games—but if you're going to say stupid things like "climb the hole," then I just can't take you seriously. **Return to "LXI" paragraph.**

LXIIIa

You shrink down to an appropriate size and crawl through the hole. When on the other side, your size returns to normal. **Go to "LVIII" paragraph.**

LXIIIb

No effect. **Return to "LXI" paragraph.**

LXIIIc

No effect. **Return to "LXI" paragraph.**

LXIIId

No effect. **Return to "LXI" paragraph.**

LXIIIe

No effect. **Return to "LXI" paragraph.**

LXIV

Location: Room O. It's there, in the distance, you see it. It's the treasure! It's a magnificent, golden orb. You begin your approach, but suddenly, the door behind you slams shut and blocks itself off with a purple force field. From the heavens, descends the very definition of a monster. It levitates just above the ground, eyeballing you with its one enormous eye. It puts barely any effort into moving its fat arms and legs, almost as if it were being pulled by strings. From its boar-like mouth and nose seeps a rich mixture of snot and spit. Its skin is a repulsive purple. As monstrous as it is, it speaks the words of a competent being. "How dare you enter my lair," it says, with the most chilling of voices. "You are not the first adventurer to enter here, and you will not be the last. Thankfully, I have grown quite adept at dispelling unwanted guests." The monster reveals a necklace of bones around its neck. It licks its lips menacingly. The door has locked itself, so you can't go back, and the monster is guarding the treasure. Looks like you have no choice but to slay the beast. If you have any potions on you, I suggest you take them now. I foresee this being one heck of a fight. **Go to "Boss Battle" (page 115).**

Enemy Combat

Bat

Enemy HP: 3

Keep track of the enemy's HP and your own. If the enemy's **HP drops to zero, you win. If your HP drops to zero, you lose, and you'll have to start over from the beginning of the** game **(or a checkpoint if you've found one). If you defeat the** enemy, **mark this in "Notes" and go to "VI" paragraph (page 6).**

Round 1: Defence

The bat swoops in for an attack. What do you do?

X

You dodge the attack and take zero damage. **Apply any changes to HP and move on to "Round 1: Attack."**

W

You block the attack, but the bat's teeth still nip you slightly and you take zero-point-five damage. **Apply any changes to HP and move on to "Round 1: Attack."**

V

You counter with your sword and deal one damage to the bat. **Apply any changes to HP and move on to "Round 1: Attack."**

U

You try to run, but the bat won't allow you to escape. It bites you and you take one damage. **Apply any changes to HP and move on to "Round 1: Attack."**

Round 1: Attack

Now it's your turn to lay the smack down. However, the bat seems to be building up adrenaline. This could be dangerous, be careful. What do you do?

Z

You punch the bat square in the jaw. You've dealt zero-point-five damage to the bat and stunned it a bit. **Apply any changes to HP and move on to "Round 2: Defence."**

Y

You slash the bat with your sword and deal zero-point-five damage. **Apply any changes to HP and skip to "Round 3: Defence."**

U

You try to run, but the bat won't allow you to escape. It bites you and you take one damage. **Apply any changes to HP and skip to "Round 3: Defence."**

Round 2: Defence

The bat is a little dazed, but this doesn't stop it from attacking. What do you do?

X

You dodge the attack and take zero damage. **Apply any changes to HP and move on to "Round 2: Attack."**

W

You block the attack, but the bat's claw still manages to scratch you, and you take zero-point-five damage. **Apply any changes to HP and move on to "Round 2: Attack."**

V

You pull off a wicked counter with your sword and deal one damage to the bat. **Apply any changes to HP and move on to "Round 2: Attack."**

U

You try to run, but the bat won't allow you to escape. It bites you and you take one damage. **Apply any changes to HP and move on to "Round 2: Attack."**

Round 2: Attack

All right, now it's your turn. You've got this, right? What do you do?

Z

You throw a good, clean punch at the bat and deal zero-point-five damage. **Apply any changes to HP and move on to "Round 3: Defence."**

Y

You strike with your sword and deal one damage to the bat. **Apply any changes to HP and move on to "Round 3: Defence."**

U

You try to run, but the bat won't allow you to escape. It bites you and you take one damage. **Apply any changes to HP and move on to "Round 3: Defence."**

Round 3: Defence

The bat seems to be more energized. This might make it harder to dodge its attacks, though this also makes the bat less focused. What do you do?

X

You try to dodge, but you're not fast enough. The bat attacks, and you take one damage. **Apply any changes to HP and move on to "Round 3: Attack."**

W

You halt the bat's swift movements by blocking, and as a result, take zero damage. **Apply any changes to HP and move on to "Round 3: Attack."**

V

You counter with your sword and deal zero-point-five damage. But the bat still manages to get in a good hit, so you also take one damage. **Apply any changes to HP and move on to "Round 3: Attack."**

U

You try to run, but the bat won't allow you to escape. It bites you and you take one damage. **Apply any changes to HP and move on to "Round 3: Attack."**

Round 3: Attack

It seems the bat's energy is returning to normal, but you're starting to get puffed out, so I suggest wrapping this up quickly. What do you do?

Z

You give the bat a good uppercut and deal zero-point-five damage. **Apply any changes to HP and move on to "Round 4: Defence."**

Y

You present some fancy swordsmanship and deal one damage to the bat. **Apply any changes to HP and move on to "Round 4: Defence."**

U

You try to run, but the bat won't allow you to escape. It bites you and you take one damage. **Apply any changes to HP and move on to "Round 4: Defence."**

Round 4: Defence

You're getting tired from all this fighting, but it doesn't look like the bat feels the same way. You need to finish this fast. Be careful. What do you do?

X

Your dodge completely fails, and you take two damage from the bat's attack. **Apply any changes to HP and move on to "Round 4: Attack."**

W

You're too tired to block properly, and you take one damage. **Apply any changes to HP and move on to "Round 4: Attack."**

V

Your counter doesn't go quite as planned and you take two damage. But you still manage to nip the bat slightly with your sword, so you also deal zero-point-five damage. **Apply any changes to HP and move on to "Round 4: Attack."**

U

You try to run but you're just too tired. The bat lands a powerful attack on you, and you take two damage. **Apply any changes to HP and move on to "Round 4: Attack."**

Round 4: Attack

Okay, here's your chance. End this quickly before you lose your life to a bat. What do you do?

Z

Ha ha ha, you missed! Ahem, I mean … oh no, you miss and deal zero damage because of it. **Apply any changes to HP and move on to "Round 5: Defence."**

Y

You land a good hit with your sword and deal one damage. **Apply any changes to HP and move on to "Round 5: Defence."**

U

Trying to run just made the bat mad and it landed a heavy attack on you. You take two damage. **Apply any changes to HP and move on to "Round 5: Defence."**

Round 5: Defence

I'll be honest with you; things aren't look too good. You need to kill this thing now, because I am not paying for your funeral. What do you do?

X

Your dodge fails and you take two damage. **Apply any changes to HP and move on to "Round 5: Attack."**

W

Your block fails and you take two damage. **Apply any changes to HP and move on to "Round 5: Attack."**

V

Your counter fails to shield you from the attack, and you take two damage. But you still get a hit of your own in and deal zero-point-five damage. **Apply any changes to HP and move on to "Round 5: Attack."**

U

You try to run, but you trip and succumb to the bat's attack. You take two damage. **Apply any changes to HP and move on to "Round 5: Attack."**

Round 5: Attack

This is your last chance; don't mess this up. What do you do?

Z

You give the bat a good old knuckle sandwich and deal zero-point-five damage. **Apply any changes to HP and move on to "Round 6: Defence."**

Y

You strike with your sword, but you miss and deal zero damage. How embarrassing. **Apply any changes to HP and move on to "Round 6: Defence."**

U

The bat won't let you leave. You take two damage. **Apply any changes to HP and move on to "Round 6: Defence."**

Round 6: Defence

I hope you have life insurance, because you are not making it out of this. What do you do?

X

Your dodge fails and you take five damage. **Go to the last paragraph in the "Bat" section.**

W

Your block fails and you take five damage. **Go to the last paragraph in the "Bat" section.**

V

Your counter fails and you take five damage. **Go to the last paragraph in the "Bat" section.**

U

You're too tired to even attempt to run. You take five damage. **Go to the last paragraph in the "Bat" section.**

At this point, if you and the bat still have HP remaining and neither of you have hit zero, then you have calculated the damages incorrectly. I suggest restarting the battle and paying closer attention to how you calculate the damages.

Giant Lizard

Enemy HP: 4

Keep track of the enemy's HP and your own. If the enemy's HP drops to zero, you win. If your HP drops to zero, you lose, and you'll have to start over from the beginning of the game (or a checkpoint if you've found one). If you defeat the enemy, mark this in "Notes" and return to "XXI" paragraph (page 23).

Round 1: Attack

You ready yourself to strike the first blow. What do you do?

Z

You punch the lizard and deal one damage, but it's fast and manages to bite you as well. You take zero-point-five damage. **Apply any changes to HP and move on to "Round 1: Defence."**

Y

You land a decent hit with your sword and deal zero-point-five damage. **Apply any changes to HP and move on to "Round 1: Defence."**

U

Your escape is successful. **Return to "XXI" paragraph (page 23).**

Round 1: Defence

The lizard is preparing to attack. It seems really fast, so be careful. What do you do?

X

You weren't fast enough to dodge the attack. You take two damage. **Apply any changes to HP and move on to "Round 2: Attack."**

W

You successfully block the attack a receive zero damage. **Apply any changes to HP and move on to "Round 2: Attack."**

V

You counter the attack with your sword and deal zero-point-five damage to the lizard, but it bites you, and you take zero-point-five damage. **Apply any changes to HP and move on to "Round 2: Attack."**

U

Your escape is successful. **Return to "XXI" paragraph (page 23).**

Round 2: Attack

Now it's your turn to attack. Remember that some attacks will work better on some monster than on others. What do you do?

Z

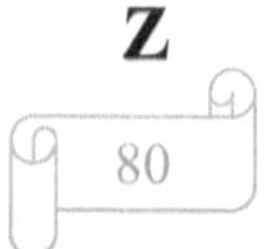

You land your punch and deal one damage. **Apply any changes to HP and move on to "Round 2: Defence."**

Y

You attack with your sword and deal zero-point-five damage. But this doesn't stop the lizard from biting you. You also take one damage. **Apply any changes to HP and move on to "Round 2: Defence."**

U

Your escape is successful. **Return to "XXI" paragraph (page 23).**

Round 2: Defence

Remember how fast the lizard is. What do you do?

X

Your dodge fails and you take two damage. **Apply any change to HP and move on to "Round 3: Attack."**

W

Your block fails and take one damage. **Apply any changes to HP and move on to "Round 3: Attack."**

V

You counter the attack and deal one damage to the lizard. A critical hit! **Apply any changes to HP and move on to "Round 3: Attack."**

U

Your escape is successful. **Return to "XXI" paragraph (page 23).**

Round 3: Attack

All right, it's your turn; you know what to do. What do you do?

Z

You punch and land a critical hit. That's two damage, lucky you! **Apply any changes to HP and move on to "Round 3: Defence."**

Y

The lizard blocks your attack and counters with a swinging tail. You take one damage. **Apply any changes to HP and move on to "Round 3: Defence."**

U

Your escape is successful. **Return to "XXI" paragraph (page 23).**

Round 3: Defence

You're looking kind of tired, but the lizard isn't. Better wrap this up quickly. What do you do?

X

You weren't fast enough to dodge the attack. You take two damage. **Apply any changes to HP and move on to "Round 4: Attack."**

W

Your block was successful but not the best. The lizard nipped your arm, and you take zero-point-five damage. **Apply any changes to HP and move on to "Round 4: Attack."**

V

You counter and deal zero-point-five damage. Apply any changes to HP and move on to "Round 4: Attack."

U

Your escape is successful. **Return to "XXI" paragraph (page 23).**

Round 4: Attack

Don't push yourself too hard. Remember, you can't last as long as the monsters in here can. Let's end this fast. What do you do?

Z

You throw a punch and deal zero-point-five damage. However, this attack is reckless and the lizard counters. You also take one damage. **Apply any changes to HP and move on to "Round 4: Defence."**

Y

You lunge your sword, but you are clearly getting very tired. You miss and do zero damage. **Apply any changes to HP and move on to "Round 4: Defence."**

U

Your escape is successful. **Return to "XXI" paragraph (page 23).**

Round 4: Defence

I don't think this is going well for you. Guess I'll start making funeral preparations. What do you do?

X

Your dodge fails miserably, and you take two damage. **Apply any changes to HP and move on to "Round 5: Attack."**

W

Your block fails and you take one damage. **Apply any changes to HP and move on to "Round 5: Attack."**

V

Your counter is weak, but successful. You take one damage, but you deal zero-point-five damage. **Apply any changes to HP and move on to "Round 5: Attack."**

U

Your escape is successful. **Return to "XXI" paragraph (page 23).**

Round 5: Attack

I hope you've written a will. If not, then I'm taking your stuff, deal? What do you do?

Z

You miss and the lizard counters. You take two damage. **Apply any changes to HP and move on to "Round 5: Defence."**

Y

You land a weak attack with your sword and deal zero-point-five damage. **Apply any changes to HP and move on to "Round 5: Defence."**

U

Your escape is successful. **Return to "XXI" paragraph (page 23).**

Round 5: Defence

Let's be honest, you're not going to make it. Is there anyone you'd like me to call for you? What do you do?

X

You're too tired to dodge, and so you are hit with an attack and take five damage. **Go to the last paragraph in the "Giant Lizard" section.**

W

You're too tired to block and you take five damage. **Go to the last paragraph in the "Giant Lizard" section.**

V

Your counter fails and you take five damage. **Go to the last paragraph in the "Giant Lizard" section.**

U

Your escape is successful. **Return to "XXI" paragraph (page 23).**

At this point, if you and the giant lizard still have HP remaining and neither of you have hit zero, then you have calculated the damages incorrectly. I suggest restarting the battle and paying closer attention to how you calculate the damages.

Spider

Enemy HP: 1

Keep track of the enemy's HP and your own. If the enemy's HP drops to zero, you win. If your HP drops to zero, you lose, and you'll have to start over from the beginning of the game (or a checkpoint if you've found one). If you defeat the enemy, mark this in "Notes" and return to "XXXIII" paragraph (page 36).

Round 1: Attack

I don't know about this. This thing looks pretty tough. What do you do?

Z

You punch the spider, and you're lucky you didn't break your hand. The spider took no damage at all! **Apply any changes to HP and move on to "Round 1: Defence."**

Y

Your sword just bounces off. The spider takes no damage whatsoever. **Apply any changes to HP and move on to "Round 1: Defence."**

U

Your escape is successful. **Return to "XXXIII" paragraph (page 36).**

Round 1: Defence

Well, okay then. You've dealt a total of … let me see here … zero damage. This one's strong. Maybe we should call it quits. What do you do?

X

Wow, this thing's way faster than you. Oh, uh, your dodge failed, by the way, and you take two damage. **Apply any changes to HP and move on to "Round 2: Attack."**

W

You try to block and—Oh, my gosh, are you okay? This thing is kicking your butt. I hate to say it, but you took two damage. **Apply any changes to HP and move on to "Round 2: Attack."**

V

Well, you tried … and you failed laughably. You take two damage. **Apply any changes to HP and move on to "Round 2: Attack."**

U

Your escape is successful. **Return to "XXXIII" paragraph (page 36).**

Round 2: Attack

Okay, I'm gonna be real with you, I don't think you're gonna make it … unless you run—now. Listen to me, please. What do you do?

Z

Nope, you missed. **Apply any changes to HP and move on to "Round 2: Defence."**

Y

Your sword didn't do a thing. **Apply any changes to HP and move on to "Round 2: Defence."**

U

Your escape is successful. **Return to "XXXIII" paragraph (page 36).**

Round 2: Defence

Look, I really don't want to deal with all your loved ones when you're gone. Just quit now, there'll be another time. What do you do?

X

You take two damage. No, I'm not even going to tell you what happened … it would only make you cry. **Apply any changes to HP and move on to "Round 3: Attack."**

W

Do I even have to say it? You take two damage. **Apply any changes to HP and move on to "Round 3: Attack."**

V

You'd think countering would work, but you'd be wrong. You take two damage. **Apply any changes to HP and move on to "Round 3: Attack."**

U

Your escape is successful. **Return to "XXXIII" paragraph (page 36).**

Round 3: Attack

Come on, it's just not gonna happen today. Maybe you can find a weapon that'll work better. Don't die here! What do you do?

Z

You deal zero damage. You're just not a match for this thing. **Apply any changes to HP and move on to "Round 3: Defence."**

Y

Please just select the "Run" option. Come on, I'm breaking the fourth wall for you. Please, listen to me. Oh, and you take two damage. **Apply any changes to HP and move on to "Round 3: Defence."**

U

Your escape is successful. **Return to "XXXIII" paragraph (page 36).**

Round 3: Defence

Run away! Run away! For the love of all that is good, please run away! What do you do?

X

Before you can do anything, the spider crushes you with one, huge leg. You take five damage. **Go to the last paragraph in the "Spider" section.**

W

Before you can do anything, the spider crushes you with one, huge leg. You take five damage. **Go to the last paragraph in the "Spider" section.**

V

Before you can do anything, the spider crushes you with one, huge leg. You take five damage. **Go to the last paragraph in the "Spider" section.**

U

Your escape is successful. **Return to "XXXIII" paragraph (page 36).**

At this point, if you and the spider still have HP remaining and neither of you have hit zero, then you have calculated the

damages incorrectly. I suggest restarting the battle and paying closer attention to how you calculate the damages.

Giant Lizard 2

Enemy HP: 3

Keep track of the enemy's HP and your own. If the enemy's HP drops to zero, you win. If your HP drops to zero, you lose, and you'll have to start over from the beginning of the game (or a checkpoint if you've found one). If you defeat the enemy, mark this in "Notes" and return to "XLV" paragraph (page 48).

Round 1: Defence

Well, hey, you win some, you lose some, right? Just do your best, okay? What do you do?

X

Nice dodge. You take zero damage. **Apply any changes to HP and move on to "Round 1: Attack."**

W

Looks like your block failed. You take two damage. **Apply any changes to HP and move on to "Round 1: Attack."**

V

Whoa, careful! Not the best counter, but it seems to have worked. You take one-point-five damage, but you also deal one damage. **Apply any changes to HP and move on to "Round 1: Attack."**

U

You try to run, but the lizard blocks you path and swipes at you. You take one damage. **Apply any changes to HP and move on to "Round 1: Attack."**

Round 1: Attack

Okay, your turn. Let's take it to 'em! What do you do?

Z

You punch the lizard and deal zero-point-five damage. You also manage to stun the enemy. Yay! **Apply any changes to HP and skip to "Round 2: Attack."**

Y

You attack with your sword. Hiyah! You deal one damage. **Apply any changes to HP and move on to "Round 2: Defence."**

U

You try to run, but the lizard blocks you path and swipes at you. You take one damage. **Apply any changes to HP and move on to "Round 2: Defence."**

Round 2: Defence

Hmm, seems lizzy's got a bit more vigor. Be careful. What do you do?

X

Wow, it's fast. Your dodge was unsuccessful, and you take two-point-five damage. **Apply any changes to HP and move on to "Round 2: Attack."**

W

Your block lessens the damage, but it doesn't outright stop it. You take one-point-five damage. **Apply any changes to HP and move on to "Round 2: Attack."**

V

You execute an okay counter. You take one damage, but you also deal zero-point-five damage. **Apply any changes to HP and move on to "Round 2: Attack."**

U

You try to run, but the lizard blocks you path and swipes at you. You take one damage. **Apply any changes to HP and move on to "Round 2: Attack."**

Round 2: Attack

Whoa, looks like it's slowing down a little. Do you think it overexerted itself? What do you do?

Z

You throw a punch, but you miss—tragic! You deal zero damage. **Apply any changes to HP and move on to "Round 3: Defence."**

Y

You land a clean hit with your sword and deal one damage. **Apply any changes to HP and move on to "Round 3: Defence."**

U

You try to run, but the lizard blocks your path and swipes at you. You take one damage. **Apply any changes to HP and move on to "Round 3: Defence."**

Round 3: Defence

The lizard looks a little tuckered out now. This might be your chance to hit it with some strong attacks, but first, you've got to defend. What do you do?

X

That was a great dodge. You take zero damage. **Apply any changes to HP and move on to "Round 3: Attack."**

W

You block the lizards pathetic attack and take zero damage because of it. **Apply any changes to HP and move on to "Round 3: Attack."**

V

Wow! Critical hit! But the lizard still manages to get you. You take one damage and deal one-point-five damage. Great job! (Yes, I give compliment … on occasion.) **Apply any changes to HP and move on to "Round 3: Attack."**

U

You try to run, but the lizard blocks your path and swipes at you. You take one damage. **Apply any changes to HP and move on to "Round 3: Attack."**

Round 3: Attack

Now's your chance. It still looks a little tired. Hit 'em with something strong!

Z

Your punch misses and you deal zero damage. **Apply any changes to HP and move on to "Round 4: Defence."**

Y

You get in a spectacular hit with your sword. That's one damage dealt. **Apply any changes to HP and move on to "Round 4: Defence."**

U

You try to run, but the lizard blocks you path and swipes at you. You take one damage. **Apply any changes to HP and move on to "Round 4: Defence."**

Round 4: Defence

You're looking a bit tired. Better finish this up quickly. Remember, monsters have way more endurance than you do. What do you do?

X

You didn't dodge fast enough. You take three damage. **Apply any changes to HP and move on to "Round 4: Attack."**

W

The lizard tears through your block and you take one damage. **Apply any changes to HP and move on to "Round 4: Attack."**

V

Your counter didn't work too well. You take two damage, but you managed to graze the lizard with the counter and deal zero-point-five damage. **Apply any changes to HP and move on to "Round 4: Attack."**

U

You try to run, but the lizard blocks you path and swipes at you. You take one damage. **Apply any changes to HP and move on to "Round 4: Attack."**

Round 4: Attack

I'll be honest, there's a ninety percent chance you're going to die here. Anyone you need me to call, or are you good? What do you do?

Z

You miss and suffer a powerful counterattack. You take three damage. **Apply any changes to HP and move on to "Round 5: Defence."**

Y

You manage a slight scrape with your sword and deal zero-point-five damage, but the lizard counters and you take two damage. **Apply any changes to HP and move on to "Round 5: Defence."**

U

You try to run, but the lizard blocks your path and swipes at you. You take one damage. **Apply any changes to HP and move on to "Round 5: Defence."**

Round 5: Defence

This is it. You're dead. I'm going on holiday, so see ya. What do you do?

X

That dodge was laughably bad, and it failed too. You take five damage. **Go to the last paragraph in the "Giant Lizard 2" section.**

W

You couldn't execute the block in time. You take five damage. **Go to the last paragraph in the "Giant Lizard 2" section.**

V

Your counter fails and you take five damage. **Go to the last paragraph in the "Giant Lizard 2" section.**

U

You try to run, but the lizard blocks you path and swipes at you with a critical blow. You take five damage. **Go to the last paragraph in the "Giant Lizard 2" paragraph.**

At this point, if you and the giant lizard still have HP remaining and neither of you have hit zero, then you have calculated the damages incorrectly. I suggest restarting the battle and paying closer attention to how you calculate the damages.

Conversations

Ostrich

Read what the ostrich says, then read and select either A, B, or C (or any variants) depending on what you want to do. After that, read the corresponding response. E.g. if you pick "A," then read the ostrich's "A" response.

Start

"Ugh, my stomach," the ostrich says. It looks at you. "Who are you?" What do you do?

Your Responses

A

Introduce yourself.

B

Say, "Holy Hannah, you can talk?"

C

Say, "Is this conversation going to be long? I have a temple to explore."

Ostrich's "A" Response

"That's an odd name. What do you want?" The ostrich takes a second to crouch in pain. What do you do?

Your Responses

A1

Say, "Need some help?"

A2

Say, "My name's not odd!"

Ostrich's "B" Response

"Yes, I can talk. Obviously! What, you think just because I'm an ostrich I don't have a grasp on the English language? That's racist!" It shakes its head in derision. What do you do?

Your Responses

B1

Say, "Sorry, I didn't mean to offend you."

B2

Say, "It was just a question. Jeez, don't be so sensitive."

Ostrich's "C" Response

"If you don't want to talk to me then fine, don't talk." The ostrich gives you a dirty look. **Return to "X" paragraph (page 10).**

Ostrich's "A1" Response

"I haven't eaten in days. I'm starving. Do you think … maybe … you could get me some food?" What do you do?

Your Responses

A3

Say, "I'm on it!"

A4

Say, "Doesn't really sound like a good use of my time."

Ostrich's "A2" Response

"It's not odd to you, you're a human. But to my ears, it's not a very ostrich-y name." What do you do?

Your Responses

A5

Say, "Anyway, is there something I can help you with?" **If you say this, go to "Ostrich's 'A1' Response."**

A6

Say, "Of course it's not an ostrich-y name. Do I look like an ostrich to you? Look, do you need help or not?"

Ostrich's "B1" Response

"Too late, I'm offended." The ostrich groans in pain. "Hey, if you want to make amends, you could find me some food. I'm starving." What do you do?

Your Responses

B3

Say, "Say no more," and place a big inviting smile on your face.

B4

Say, "Sounds like a waste of time. Get your own food."

Ostrich's "B2" Response

"Sensitive? How could you say that? I'm not sensitive, your sensitive." The ostrich looks away. "I'm done with this conversation!" **Return to "X" paragraph (page 10).**

Ostrich's "A3" Response

"Thank you. You're nice." **Return to "X" paragraph (page 10).**

Ostrich's "A4" Response

"Fine, don't help. You're too selfish for my liking anyway." **Return to "X" paragraph (page 10).**

Ostrich's "A6" Response

"You are rude. If you want to help, then get me some food, if not, leave me alone." **Return to "X" paragraph (page 10).**

Ostrich's "B3" Response

"Thank you. I knew I'd be able to count on you." **Return to "X" paragraph (page 10).**

Ostrich's "B4" Response

"Fine, don't help me. I don't need your help anyway. And … you're ugly too!" The ostrich won't look at you anymore. It seems this conversation is over. **Return to "X" paragraph (page 10).**

Old Man

Read what the old man says, then read and select either A, B, or C (or any variants) depending on what you want to do. After that, read the corresponding response. E.g. if you pick "A," then read the old man's "A" response.

Start

"Well, what brings you to this temple, young one?" the old man says. What do you do?

Your Responses

A

Say, "None of your business, old man!"

B

Say, "I'm looking for treasure."

C

Say, "Sorry, I didn't realise this was going to be a conversation. I don't have time for this."

Old Man's "A" Response

"Ha ha ha! No, I suppose it isn't. All right then, carry on." **Return to "XXX" paragraph (page 33).**

Old Man's "B" Response

"Are you now? Well, you know what they say: it's dangerous when you're lonesome, so take this. (I think that's right)." **The old man gives you a potion. Mark this in "Notes." Return to "XXX" paragraph (page 33).**

Old Man's "C" Response

"Not a problem, I understand. I'll be here if you change your mind." **Return to "XXX" paragraph (page 33).**

Puzzles

Button Puzzle

Answer: 2, 4, 3, 1

If you wrote down the correct sequence of numbers, then the door (XXVII) is now open. Mark this in "Notes" and return to "XXV" paragraph (page 27). If you did not write the sequence as shown, you take two damage, and the door remains locked. Apply these changes to HP and return to "XXV" paragraph (page 27).

Mysterious Writing

Answer: Red

If you answered correctly, then your prize gently floats down to you. It is a Bow & Arrow. Mark this in "Notes" and draw a checkmark next to the item. You hear a voice that says: "A Bow & Arrow is a powerful weapon that some monsters have a weakness to. But it's not just a weapon. Try it out on many things and see what happens." Upon receiving the Bow & Arrow, you also get a checkpoint. Draw a horizontal line in "Notes" to mark this. Now, if you die, you can start your adventure again from this point ("XXXVIII" paragraph). Everything coming before the line you've drawn will remain, even if you die. But anything coming after the line, if you die, will be lost and you'll have to acquire them again. If you did not answer the puzzle correctly, you take two damage and do not get a checkpoint or the Bow & Arrow. Apply any changes to HP and return to "XXXVIII" paragraph (page 41).

Switch Puzzle

Answer: 1

If you answered correctly then the door (XLVI) is now unlocked. Mark this in "Notes" and return to "XLV" paragraph (page 48). If you answered incorrectly, then you are attacked by a giant lizard. If this is the case, go to "Giant Lizard 2" in the "Enemy Combat" section (page 93).

Boss Battle

Conversation

Read what the boss says, then read and select either A, B, or C (or any variants) depending on what you want to do. After that, read the corresponding response. E.g. if you pick "A," then read the boss's "A" response.

Start

"Well, well, well, I congratulate you for making it this far. My name is Kowaionna." The frightening figure looks at the treasure behind itself, and then back at you. "You want the treasure, don't you? Well, you'll have to go through me to get it, and trust me, you will not have the opportunity to slay me. When you are dead, I shall very much enjoy prying the flesh off your tiny bones."

Your Responses

A

Say, "Y-y-you're kinda scary. I don't know if I can do this."

B

Say nothing and prepare for battle.

C

Say, "Shut up and move, pig. That treasure is mine, and I'm taking it whether you like it or not."

Boss's "A" Response

"You scaredy cat … pathetic! Grow a backbone!" It throws a lightning bolt your way and you take one damage. **Apply any changes to HP and move on to "Puzzle" in the "Boss Battle" section.**

Boss's "B" Response

"I see you prefer actions to words. Very well, let the battle begin." **Move on to "Puzzle" in the "Boss Battle" section.**

Boss's "C" Response

"How rude! Your parents would have been wise to put a muzzle on their spawn. Enough talking! Now, we fight!" It throws a lightning bolt your way and you take two damage. **Apply any changes to HP and move on to "Puzzle" in the "Boss Battle" section.**

Puzzle

It's time to fight. I hope you're ready for this. Uh-oh, looks like that ugly pig is starting to project a force field. I don't think it should be too difficult for you to break through though. You're pretty good with a sword (don't let it go to your head).

Huh? You can't move? What do you mean? Well, figure it out, you're a sitting duck just standing there! "Answer the riddles." … What was that? "Answer the riddles, and you shall move once again." Oh great, your survival relies on your brain power. Well, guess it's funeral time. **Attempt each riddle one by one. Do not move on to the next one until you have answered the one before. Read the riddles carefully, there are always clues hidden within them. Once you think you have the answer, check the "Puzzle Answers" section (on the page after the "Puzzle" section of the "Boss Battle" section) to see if you are correct. If you are, move on to the next riddle, if you are not, you will take one damage (for each incorrect answer), but you may still continue to the next riddle.**

Riddle #1

The voice speaks: "Leprechauns are the same as elves, don't you think? With that in mind, what is a leprechaun's favourite colour?" **When you have the answer, check it in the "Puzzle Answers" section.**

Riddle #2

The voice speaks: "I'm thinking of just four numbers. You probably already know them. Why am I thinking of numbers? I don't know. I am a little bit … backwards today." **When you have the answer, check it in the "Puzzle Answers" section.**

Riddle #3

The voice speaks: "The numbers are: 3, 5, 4, and 2. What am I talking about? I won't tell you. It's … the name of the game." **When you have the answer, check it in the "Puzzle Answers" section.**

Riddle #1 Answer

A Leprechaun's favourite colour is red. **If you answered correctly, try to answer "Riddle #2." If you were incorrect, you take one damage, but you may still proceed to "Riddle #2."**

Riddle #2 Answer

The answer is: 1, 3, 4, 2. **If you answered correctly, try to answer "Riddle #3." If you were incorrect, you take one damage, but you may still proceed to "Riddle #3."**

Riddle #3 Answer

The answer is: nice. **If you answered incorrectly, you take one damage, and if you were correct, you take no damage. Continue to the "Combat" section (in the "Boss Battle" section).**

Combat

All right, you can move again! (I didn't think you were going to get out of that one). Huh? No, I didn't say anything. Anyway, let's skip through the non-interactive stuff. Let's see … you howl into the air, pounding your chest … oops, wrong script. Uh, right, so … you take down the force field with your sword and finally get to battle this thing fairly (or as close to fair as you can get). **If you decided to feed the ostrich and have become its friend, go to "Battle 2" in the "Boss Battle" section. If you did not make friends with the ostrich, go to "Battle 1" in the "Boss Battle" section.**

Battle 1

Enemy HP: 3

I'm going to say this once: BE CAREFUL! This is the FINAL BOSS, and it's not a pushover. This won't be like that game where the plumber guy just cuts the bridge with an axe to drown the big turtle guy in lava and win. (I know, I totally love that game too, but this ain't that, kid). **Keep track of the boss's HP and your own. If the boss's HP drops to zero, you win. If your HP drops to zero, you lose, and you'll have to start over from the beginning of the game (or a checkpoint if you've found one). If you defeat the boss, then congratulations. Go to "Ending 1" (Page 137).**

Round 1: Attack

All right, you've got the first move. Make it count, buddy. What do you do?

Z

You start with a punch to that ugly mug, but it didn't really work. That's zero damage dealt. **Apply any changes to HP and move on to "Round 1: Defence."**

Y

Coming in strong with a blade to the face, eh? Good choice. That's one damage. **Apply any changes to HP and move on to "Round 1: Defence."**

U

A lightning bolt stops you from escaping. You take one damage. **Apply any changes to HP and move on to "Round 1: Defence."**

Round 1: Defence

Remember what I said before? I won't say it again. You know what to do. What do you do?

X

Whoa, this thing's faster than I thought (that, or your dodge was just atrocious). Anyway, you just received a blow to the head and take three damage. **Apply any changes to HP and move on to "Round 2: Attack."**

W

All right, block successful! You took zero damage. **Apply any changes to HP and move on to "Round 2: Attack."**

V

Well, guess you can't win 'em all. You take three damage for a bad counterattack. **Apply any changes to HP and move on to "Round 2: Attack."**

U

A lightning bolt stops you from escaping. You take one damage. **Apply any changes to HP and move on to "Round 2: Attack."**

Round 2: Attack

Not much I can offer in advice right now. Just do you best, okay? (And pray that's enough). What do you do?

Z

Wow, nice hit. Punching isn't usually that effective on a monster … lucky you! You deal one damage. **Apply any changes to HP and move on to "Round 2: Defence."**

Y

You attack with your trusty sword. Hmm … it didn't seem to work though. You deal zero damage. **Apply any changes to HP and move on to "Round 2: Defence."**

U

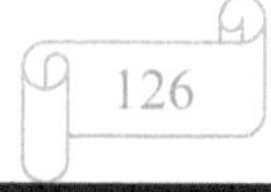

A lightning bolt stops you from escaping. You take one damage. **Apply any changes to HP and move on to "Round 2: Defence."**

Round 2: Defence

Hmm, I wonder if it's possible to alternate one's weaknesses. Sorry, that was a little off-topic. Ignore me. What do you do?

X

Jeez, this thing's really fast, faster than you are anyway. Your dodge fails and you take three damage. **Apply any changes to HP and move on to "Round 3: Attack."**

W

You try to block but the monster tears through. You take one damage. **Apply any changes to HP and move on to "Round 3: Attack."**

V

Man, that was a bad counter. You deal zero damage. **Apply any changes to HP and move on to "Round 3: Attack."**

U

A lightning bolt stops you from escaping. You take one damage. **Apply any changes to HP and move on to "Round 3: Attack."**

Round 3: Attack

All righty, same drill as before. Take it to 'em! What do you do?

Z

You land a clean right hook and deal one damage. **Apply any changes to HP and move on to "Round 3: Defence."**

Y

You strike a hit with your blade, but it doesn't work. You deal zero damage. **Apply any changes to HP and move on to "Round 3: Defence."**

U

A lightning bolt stops you from escaping. You take one damage. **Apply any changes to HP and move on to "Round 3: Defence."**

Round 3: Defence

Wait a minute, this pig thing is starting to glow purple. You'd better end this quickly, it's not looking too good for you right now. What do you do?

X

Whoa, it's super fast now, and stronger too. Suffice to say, your dodge failed, and you take four damage. **Apply any changes to HP and move on to "Round 4: Attack."**

W

Your block is crippled by a powerful hammer arm. You take three damage. **Apply any changes to HP and move on to "Round 4: Attack."**

V

Well, the counter sort-of works and you deal zero-point-five damage, but you also get hit in the process and take one damage. **Apply any change to HP and move on to "Round 4: Attack."**

U

A lightning bolt stops you from escaping. You take one damage. **Apply any changes to HP and move on to "Round 4: Attack."**

Round 4: Attack

I'm surprised you're still alive. You've got to hurry though; I don't think you'll last much longer. What do you do?

Z

Oh no, you missed. You deal zero damage. **Apply any changes to HP and move on to "Round 4: Defence."**

Y

Nice hit. That's one damage dealt. **Apply any changes to HP and move on to "Round 4: Defence."**

U

A lightning bolt stops you from escaping. You take one damage. **Apply any changes to HP and move on to "Round 4: Defence."**

Round 4: Defence

Please don't die. Please don't die. Please don't die. What do you do?

X

Your dodge was laughably bad. You take three damage. **Apply any changes to HP and move on to "Round 5: Attack."**

W

Your block deflected absolutely nothing. You take three damage. **Apply any changes to HP and move on to "Round 5: Attack."**

V

That counter could not have been any worse. You take three damage. **Apply any changes to HP and move on to "Round 5: Attack."**

U

A lightning bolt stops you from escaping. You take one damage. **Apply any changes to HP and move on to "Round 5: Attack."**

Round 5: Attack

You have one chance. If you fail, well … let's think happy thoughts. What do you do?

Z

A weak hit, but it did the job. You deal zero-point-five damage. **Apply any changes to HP and move on the "Round 5: Defence."**

Y

Your attack misses. That means zero damage dealt. Dang. **Apply any changes to HP and move on to "Round 5: Defence."**

U

A lightning bolt stops you from escaping. You take one damage. **Apply any changes to HP and move on to "Round 5: Defence."**

Round 5: Defence

So, just before you die, you'll will all your stuff to me, right? What do you do?

X

You take five damage. It's … to bad to describe. **Apply any changes to HP and move on to the last paragraph in the "Boss Battle: Battle 1" section.**

W

Oh … that looks bad. Are you okay? You take five damage. **Apply any changes to HP and move on to the last paragraph in the "Boss Battle: Battle 1" section.**

V

It knocked your sword away—uh-oh. You take five damage. **Apply any changes to HP and move on to the last paragraph in the "Boss Battle: Battle 1" section.**

U

A lightning bolt stops you from escaping. You take five damage. **Apply any changes to HP and move on to the last paragraph in the "Boss Battle: Battle 1" section.**

At this point, if you and the boss still have HP remaining and neither of you have hit zero, then you have calculated the damages incorrectly. I suggest restarting the battle and paying closer attention to how you calculate the damages.

Battle 2

Enemy HP: 2

All right, you can move again. Time to kick some butt. Wait, what's that sound? An increasingly loud thumping sound is followed by a foot kicking the locked door open again. When the purple smoke clears, you see it. It's … the purple ostrich!? (Okay, let's just go with it.) "Don't hurt my friend, you pork face!" it says. It dashes to the monster and feeds it a flurry of foot-attacks (do ostriches even have feet? Talons, maybe? Oh, whatever). The ostrich fights, but it can't fight forever. The monster smacks the ostrich, and it falls. It's not dead, but it won't be fighting anymore. Looks like the rest is up to you. Good thing the ostrich weakened it, huh? **Keep track of the boss's HP and your own. If the boss's HP drops to zero, you win. If your HP drops to zero, you lose, and you'll have to start over from the beginning of the game (or a checkpoint if you've found one). If you defeat the boss, then congratulations. Go to "Ending 2" (page 138).**

Round 1: Attack

Right, let's do this! I believe in you. (What did I just say?) What do you do?

Z

Great hit. You deal one damage. **Apply any changes to HP and move on to "Round 1: Defence."**

Y

Good hit, I bet that hurt it. You deal one damage. **Apply any changes to HP and move on to "Round 1: Defence."**

U

A lightning bolt stops you from escaping. You take one damage. **Apply any changes to HP and move on to "Round 1: Defence."**

Round 1: Defence

Don't let your guard down. It may be weakened, but this thing is a boss for a reason. What do you do?

X

Great job! You dodged successfully and received zero damage. **Apply any changes to HP and move on to "Round 2: Attack."**

W

You block, but you're not strong enough to hold it. You take four damage. **Apply any changes to HP and move on to "Round 2: Attack."**

V

You counter and deal zero-point-five damage, but this doesn't stop you from getting hit in the process. You also receive three damage. **Apply any changes to HP and move on to "Round 2: Attack."**

U

A lightning bolt stops you from escaping. You take one damage. **Apply any changes to HP and move on to "Round 2: Attack."**

Round 2: Attack

Okay, you're doing well. Keep it going. What do you do?

Z

You land a clean uppercut (like those completely over-the-top anime ones). You deal one damage. **Apply any changes to HP and move on to "Round 2: Defence."**

Y

You land a double-handed sword slash and deal one-point-five damage. **Apply any changes to HP and move on to "Round 2: Defence."**

U

A lightning bolt stops you from escaping. You take one damage. **Apply any changes to HP and move on to "Round 2: Defence."**

Round 2: Defence

Uh-oh, what's happening? This pig monster's vibrating … and its eyes are starting to glow. I've … gotta write you a will. Don't worry, this is just in case. I'll just will all your stuff to me, okay? What do you do?

X

Holy moly, are you okay? Eww, that doesn't look good. You take five damage. **Apply any changes to HP and move on to the last paragraph in the "Boss Battle: Battle 2" section.**

W

Oh, no! Get up, your still in this. Oh, you're not moving. You take five damage. **Apply any changes to HP and move on to the last paragraph in the "Boss Battle: Battle 2" section.**

V

… Uh, do I have to describe this? It's a bit … gruesome. You take five damage. **Apply any changes to HP and move on to the last paragraph in the "Boss Battle: Battle 2" section.**

U

A lightning bolt stops you from escaping. You take five damage. **Apply any changes to HP and move on to the last paragraph in the "Boss Battle: Battle 2" section.**

At this point, if you and the boss still have HP remaining and neither of you have hit zero, then you have calculated the damages incorrectly. I suggest restarting the battle and paying closer attention to how you calculate the damages.

Ending 1

You did it … you actually did it. You defeated the boss. Wow, okay, guess I should finish this up then. This part of the script was never finalized, nobody actually expected you to win … no offence.

Ahem, anyway … you take the treasure, as its golden shine glistens in your hands. There is only one thing left to do now: time to collect. You leave the more-terrifying-than-expected temple behind and set out for town. Once in town, you meet up with the people who hired you (three thuggish-looking guys, but you don't discriminate). You present them with the treasure and kindly ask for your pay. The three guys look at each other and then gang up on you, beating you to the ground and taking the treasure. They laugh and walk away, leaving you on the ground, heavily beaten.

Now, you may be wondering how they beat you to the ground when you have a sword and could easily have kicked their butts. To that I say: stuff happens. What are you talking about? This is a perfectly well-written script. Look, the point is, you had fun. Isn't that why you're playing this game in the first place? Who cares that you didn't get paid, and you lost the treasure, and you've been beaten and humiliated, and as soon as you get someone to take you to the hospital, that bill is gonna be HUGE? In the end, you still had fun, right? (It's rhetorical, don't answer.) Well, anyway, game's done, so I can get paid and go home now, see ya!

Ending 2

You did it! Well … the ostrich did most of the work. It seems to have taken a liking to you though. Good thing you gave it that food earlier, huh?

You take the treasure, as its golden shine glistens in your hands. Then, the ostrich tells you to hop on and the two of you ride back to town to collect your pay (I guess the ostrich is feeling better after the beating it just took). Once in town, you meet up with the three thuggish-looking guys who hired you. You offer up the treasure and kindly ask for your pay. However, one of the guys says: "You know, I was thinking that maybe there's a way we can get that treasure for free." The three guys try to attack, but the ostrich scares them off by saying: "Sure you want to do that, punks?" The three of them run away screaming: "Help! Demon ostrich!" Hmm … it seems one of them dropped his wallet. You take it. Wow, that's a whole lot of money. I don't think they'll mind if you keep it.

So, great adventure finished, ancient treasure obtained, and tons of free money to boot. Not bad. Now to end the day, you and your ostrich friend ride off into the sunset. "I'm Lenny, by the way," says the ostrich. "You know, 'cause you never bothered to ask." Well, okay, that's the end. I'm gonna pick up my pay cheque and go home now. So … yeah, go away.

~The End~

What are you still doing here? Did you not see the big "The End" on page 139? It's over; go home. What, are you expecting an end-credit scene or something? This is a gamebook not a movie.

What's that face for? No, no, I'm done. Go do something else. I will not narrate your life. I don't get paid for that. And even if I did, I don't like you. Sorry to break it to you, but my cordial nature was just an act; it's required of me, it's in the job description. Let me make this one hundred percent clear: I DON'T LIKE YOU … Well, I mean, you're not the worst idiot I've had to narrate for but—no, I have to maintain a work-life balance. Boundaries. I just need to go home, ignore my wife and kids, sit in my recliner and read Darphopia. What? Oh, come on! Don't tell me you don't know what Darphopia is. It's fantasy, my annoyingly ignorant adventurer, good old fantasy.

Oh, my gosh, I just had a great idea. You should totally look up Darphopia. Read it and enlighten yourself … like, somewhere else though. Somewhere that's not here, you know? Oh, come on, buddy, read the room. Just go. That's it. Almost there. Just close the book. Almost. Little more. There.

Finally. I thought I'd never be rid of that ding-dong.